THE SHORT STORIES OF
FRAY ANGELICO CHAVEZ

THE SHORT STORIES OF
FRAY ANGELICO CHAVEZ

EDITED BY GENARO M. PADILLA

Published by the University of New Mexico Press
Third paperback edition, 2003

Library of Congress Cataloging-in-Publication Data
Chávez, Angélico, 1910–
The short stories of Fray Angélico Chávez

Bibliography: p.
Contents: New Mexico triptych—A Romeo and Juliet story
in early New Mexico—The bell that sang again—[etc.]
1. New Mexico—Fiction
I. Padilla, Genaro M., 1949–
II. Title
PS3505.H625A6   1987
813'.52   87-5992

ISBN 0-8263-0949-6 (cloth)
ISBN 0-8263-0950-X (pbk.)

Contents

Introduction / vii

New Mexico Triptych

The Angel's New Wings / 3

The Penitente Thief / 13

Hunchback Madonna / 27

A Romeo and Juliet Story in Early New Mexico / 37

The Bell That Sang Again / 47

The Fiddler and the Angelito / 61

The Black Ewe / 67

The Ardent Commandant / 75

Wake for Don Corsino / 91

The Lean Years / 99

A Desert Idyll / 117

The Tesuque Pony Express / 121

My Ancestor—Don Pedro / 125

The Colonel and the Santo / 131

Introduction

I

FRAY ANGELICO CHAVEZ HAS HAD A LONG AND RE-
markably distinguished career as a man of letters in New Mexico.
A retired Franciscan priest now living in Santa Fe, Chavez was
born in Wagon Mound on April 10, 1910. He attended school in
Mora, taught by the Sisters of Loretto, and when he was only
fourteen left New Mexico to follow his vocation at the St. Francis
Seminary in Cincinnati, Ohio. Five years later, in 1929, he received his Franciscan habit and, partly because he had displayed
early talent as a painter, he took the name Fra Angelico after the
medieval Italian painter, Fra Angelico da Fiesole. Years later, when
he was a mission priest in New Mexico, he painted frescoes,
murals, and restored much of the art in churches in Peña Blanca,
Santo Domingo, Cerrillos, and San Felipe. After graduating from

Duns Scotus College, Detroit, in 1933, he studied for the priest-hood in the Franciscan House of Studies in Indiana, and in 1937 returned home to New Mexico, where he was ordained in St. Francis Cathedral in Santa Fe—the first native New Mexican ordained by the Franciscan Order.

For over thirty years Fray Angelico Chavez served as a mis-sionary priest in various parishes and pueblo missions throughout New Mexico, and during World War II and the Korean War he served as a chaplain with the rank of captain in the U.S. Army. During this entire time, Chavez was also an incredibly prolific scholar whose early interest in the documentary sources of New Mexican religious, cultural, and social history led to intense archi-val activity and the publication of a number of church-related studies. The results of his investigations constitute an inventory of Hispanic New Mexico's past four centuries: *Our Lady of the Con-quest* (1948), *Origins of New Mexico Families in the Spanish Colonial Period* (1954), *Missions of New Mexico, 1776* (1956), *Archives of the Archdiocese of Santa Fe, 1678–1900* (1957), *Coronado's Friars* (1968), *The Oroz Codex* (1972), *My Penitente Land: Reflections on Spanish New Mexico* (1974), and most recently, *But Time and Chance: The Story of Padre Martínez of Taos* (1981). In addition to these book-length studies, there is a wealth of miscellaneous scholarship—articles on New Mexico events that span more than three cen-turies, biographical profiles, historiographic contributions to other books—for which Chavez deserves credit.

Although he has been widely recognized for his historical scholarship, Fray Angelico was actually a consummate poet and fictionist well before he wrote history. Already composing and publishing verse regularly as a teen-age seminarian in the 1920s, Chavez has, over a period of some fifty years, published five volumes of poetry. *Clothed with the Sun* (1939), a collection of devotional poems, was Fray Angelico's first book. Other collec-tions were to follow: *Eleven Lady Lyrics* (1945), *The Single Rose* (1948), and *The Virgin of Port Lligat* (1959), a complex meditation on the metaphysics of the nuclear age which was recognized as a "very commendable achievement" by T. S. Eliot.[1] As with his historical writing, there are also scores of poems published in magazines, Franciscan periodicals, and anthologies.

And, of course, during these many prolific decades, he has also written scores of short stories, tales, and sketches along with a historical novel, *The Lady from Toledo* (1960), based on real characters and incidents in Santa Fe's early history, 1610–80. His earliest fiction, much like his poetry, was written while he was studying at St. Francis Seminary in Cincinnati and was published in the *St. Anthony Messenger,* a periodical for which he wrote his first tale, "A Desert Idyll," a wonderful satire on ethnocentrically arrogant scholars, in 1929 and one of his last, "Wake for Don Corsino," in 1956. In 1940, *New Mexico Triptych* was published as a grouping of three stories organized in textual replica of the traditional three-panel altar screens that adorn old Hispano Catholic Churches in many New Mexican towns. Following a similar schema of the reredos, or altar screen, in 1957 Chavez published *From an Altar Screen,* a retablo of seven stories that had appeared earlier in the *Messenger* and elsewhere. Following his artistic avocation, Chavez himself made the pen-and-ink altar-screen drawings for *New Mexico Triptych,* while his good friend the well-known artist Peter Hurd did the illustrations for *From An Altar Screen.* Both collections were well received by readers and critics alike; *From an Altar Screen,* for exaple, received a favorable, if somewhat condescending, notice in the *New York Times Book Review.*[2] A few stories from these collections were widely enough recognized to be anthologized by prestigious publishers: "The Hunchback Madonna," from *New Mexico Triptych,* appeared in Roy J. Defarrari's *Joy in Reading* (New York: W. H. Sadlier, 1941), T. M. Pearce's *Southwesterners Write* (Albuquerque: University of New Mexico Press, 1946), and Philip McFarland's *Focus on Literature: America* (Boston: Houghton-Mifflin, 1978); "The Penitente Thief" found a place in Sr. Mariella Gable's *Our Father's House* (New York: Sheed and Ward, 1945); "The Fiddler and the Angelito" was published in Martha Foley's *The Best American Short Stories, 1948* (Houghton-Mifflin).

Nearly all of Chavez's early stories, some ten of which were published by his twentieth birthday in 1930, appeared under his given name, Manuel E. Chavez. One story, however, "Guitars and Adobes," a novella actually, appeared in the *St. Anthony Messenger* in eight-part serial form, strangely enough under the pen name F. Chalmers Ayers. Why he chose this particular name for himself is not clear. Perhaps like two other names he used—Arthur Chapman for "Beads" (1937) and Monica Lloyd for "Winnie the Breadwinner and St. Anthony" (1938)—it was meant to allow Chavez a certain narrational latitude. "Beads," for example, is a story narrated by "Chappy," presumably Chapman the author, that takes place in Denver, where Chappy meets Joe Sterkes, a fellow journalist he hasn't seen in over ten years.

Chavez used occasional pseudonyms, I suspect, to allow himself access to an imaginative locale in which the characters, as well as the narrator, are non-Hispano. Perhaps Chavez believed that the characters, as well as the story itself, would be more credible if composed by a non-Hispano author-narrator persona. In other tales for which he used pseudonyms the story is often set outside the world of New Mexico (one in Argentina, another in Delaware, and one in Spain). In many of these Chavez used the pseudonym, I would venture, just to be playful. One of his favorite was the female pseudonym "Ann Jellico"—a play obviously on the Anglo pronunciation of his Franciscan name. It wasn't until the late 1930s that he actually assumed the religious name Fray Angelico Chavez for all his writing.

For a period of some fifty years, then, Fray Angelico Chavez has heaped word upon word, publishing some two score scholarly and creative books and literally hundreds of articles, reviews, poems, and short stories.[3] His work has provided a rich and complex genealogy of Hispano experiences in New Mexico. Yet despite this outpouring of history, poetry, and fiction, Fray Angelico Chavez has been largely overlooked as one of the pioneers of Chicano literature in this century. Hopefully, this selection of stories will begin to resituate Chavez within a literary tradition that includes such writers as José Manuel Arrellano, Eusebio and Felipe M. Chacón, Fabiola Cabeza de Baca, Sabine Ullibarí, Denise Chávez, E. A. Mares, Nash Candelaria, and Rudolfo A. Anaya. Like these other writers, Chavez has created a fictive world inhabited by Indo-Hispano characters drawn from New Mexico's various villages and towns. The textual landscape upon which such characters act out their lives spans more than 300 years—all the way from the early 1700s to World War II. Again, like the work of his fellow *nuevo mexicano* artists, Chavez's historico-literary concentration upon his people's four-century tenure upon the landscape has produced a tableau of stories that resonate with that people's unique regional cultural, historic, religious, and socio-political consciousness.

II

On the narrative surface, Chavez's tales are genial, easy to read, written in a style that draws upon the rich resources of informal storytelling in the Hispano communities of New Mexico, as well as the more formal *cuento* tradition in the Southwest. Their oral nuance and storehouse of images, in fact, are remarkably similar to those of traditional Hispano *cuentos,* invoking as they do provincialisms, archetypal characters and situations, as well as an entire universe of magical images, dreamlike occurrences, Christian icons. Additionally, Chavez's tales reflect an allegorical structure much like that present in *cuentos morales,* meant not only for entertainment but to instill moral and social responsibility in the members of the community, especially in children. Chavez uses these traditional narrative structures for a world occupied by Hispano people in locales that, while they may literally exist, remain figurative because the characters are constructed in an allegorical mode. Like the figures in those *cuentos* collected by Juan B. Rael in the 1930s and 1940s, a few of which were recently adapted and republished by José Griego y Maestas and Rudolfo A. Anaya ("Los tres consejos," "Fabiano y Reyes," "El muchacho y el abuelito," "El indito de las cien vacas"),[4] the situations in Chavez's stories represent various human responses to an entire complex of moral and social dilemmas. Read within the context of the oral community from which they spring, these tales testify to the authority and endurance of the *cuento* tradition in Hispano culture.

Although his work may incorporate structural elements from the *cuento* tradition, as Chavez himself warns, his stories are not a "rehashing of old folk tales." What makes Chavez original is that his stories locate themselves somewhere between the allegorical *cuento* and historical fiction. In a sense, Chavez's fictive events,

taking place as they do upon an identifiable New Mexican landscape, constitute a socio-mythic world inhabited by Hispanos
tested again and again for their ability to endure, to sustain their
cultural lifeways, to preserve their customs in a society that de-
values them. They may be allegorical in narrative form, character
delineation, and action, but they also give significant, if subtle,
expression to the socially and historically constituted ethos that
underlies Hispano culture in New Mexico. To follow Chavez, just
as the "more or less exact date of each tale appears hidden somewhere in the background of each panel,"[5] so also do specific
historical and cultural issues remain hidden somewhere in the
background of each tale's morality structure. However implicit,
such issues are brought into sharper relief when Chavez's readers
are willing to probe the subtextual enunciations in such seemingly
facile stories.

Most of Chavez's stories in this collection are about human
relationships tangled in conflict, hopes diminished by life's con-
tingencies, tragic events, spiritual temptations, and moral dilemmas that, in typical allegorical fashion, are set right through a
mystic experience, often the appearance of a village patron saint,
which restores grace and clarity. Such thematics alone would
grant significance to Chavez's work, but, even so, there is a
complexity beyond the allegorical impulse in Chavez's stories that
has not been noted by critics, who have glossed over their social
content while commenting upon their "great charm . . . and droll
wisdom."[6] For it is in his fiction that Chavez's writing assumes a
distinct authority derived from an interplay among his fictive
imagination, his religious and ethical perspectives, and his scholarly knowledge of the long and troubled history of New Mexico's
intercultural, not to mention intracultural, tensions. Chavez's
collective fiction, then, often finds its generative power in the
consideration of those contending forces within Hispano culture
itself, problematic enough alone, but in the Southwest com-
pounded by the conflict between the Chicano and what Chavez in
My Penitente Land refers to as a "Philistine" American society.

Read chronologically as the settings progress from early in
the eighteenth century through the middle of the twentieth, the
stories and the village surroundings in which events occur pro-

duce a retablo of interconnected narrative panels that reconstitute a people's social and cultural evolution. In that fiction which focuses upon life before the American occupation in 1846, stories such as "A Romeo and Juliet Story in Early New Mexico," "The Bell That Sang Again," "The Black Ewe," and "The Ardent Commandant," the discord within the culture itself, especially between classes, is played out in isolated communities. These stories typically pit representatives of the upper class, a family that affects "pure" Spanish lineage, an arrogant Spanish officer sent to supervise the long-established colonists, a rich *patrón,* against families of mixed blood—mestizos (in New Mexico more generally referred to as *genízaros*), laboring villagers, or shepherds.

In "A Romeo and Juliet Story," the parents of a young woman refuse to acknowledge a certain young suitor because his family, the Armijos, "casually admitted that they were mestizos from Zacatecas" while the Baca's "claimed direct descent from a First Conquistador." Joaquin Amaya, a dark-skinned, quiet *genízaro* in "The Bell That Sang Again," confronts a Captain Pelayo, a redheaded soldier reputedly born in Spain, who has arrogantly flirted with his and other villagers' wives while ordering them about and making "occasional slurs about their own unlettered speech, or about their humble blood. . . ." An adaptation of the *cuento* about a woman who is tempted by a handsome stranger, "The Ardent Commandant" may be read as an elaboration of the misrelations between the *nuevo mexicanos* and the deceitful strangers imposed upon them by the Viceroy in Mexico City, many of whom were regarded as equal to the devil himself in their attempts to bring ruin upon the colonists. But such outsiders are not the only ones capable of deceit. The *patrón* who owns thousands of sheep as well as their shepherds in "The Black Ewe," for example, repeatedly sends one villager out to a distant range in order to maintain illicit relations with his young *genízara* wife. In this story the peonage system is exposed for its dehumanizing manipulation of the powerless, for even when the guilty lovers are discovered, it is the *genízara,* her dark hair mysteriously clipped to the skin, who bears the public burden when the *patrón* retreats unpunished to his hacienda. In each of these stories, Chavez creates an allegorical landscape upon which an imaginary resolu-

tion of intracultural class conflict is evoked, the result often of a
dreamlike, mystic occurrence that subverts the power relations
between rich and poor, externally imposed officials and self-
sufficient colonists, "Spaniard" and new world *genízaro*. Although history is allegorized (isn't it always?), Chavez dramatizes
the effects of class and race relations in a way that marks the
formation of a distinct consciousness that, I believe, Hispanos in
New Mexico would generally regard as representative of their
experience.

As the fictive landscape of Hispano life moves closer to the
present (from the American invasion of 1846, through the long
territorial period up to statehood in 1912, and beyond World War
II), the dilemmas confronting Chavez's characters are less and less
centered in an enclosed area of cultural experience and more
entangled in a complex of corrupting American influences. While
there is ultimately a sense of affirmation in the stories, they are
often haunted by a brooding tone of loss. In 1848 *los extranjeros*
seized political power in the West; subsequent to that usurpation
an entirely different system of social and economic relations was
established. The transformation was irrevocable. Land-grant
communities were dispersed. Village life was disrupted. The Hispanos' religious customs were degraded, their communal values
corrupted, their very sense of time and space systematically destroyed by the requirements of survival in the new social order.
"Wake for Don Corsino," "The Lean Years," "The Angel's New
Wings" simultaneously examine internal cultural tension and the
disruptive external influences for which the railroad, Archbishop
Lamy's clergy, and various commercial enterprises are the chief
metaphors.

Chavez's implicit criticism of his own people's failure to
watch over their traditions and cultural values is clear in much of
his fiction. "The Fiddler and the Angelito," "The Penitente
Thief," and "The Angel's New Wings" variously examine aspects
of cultural decline, whether it be an old woodcutter's impetuous
refusal to play his violin at a child's wake as he (like his father
before him) had customarily done, the gradual falling of the
penitente brotherhood, or a *santero*'s bewildered response to dis-
regarded Christmas traditions in his village. As is typical of the

cuento's didactic structure, these stories serve to remind Hispanos of their responsibility to communal custom and cultural traditions. Nevertheless, the corruptive influence of Americanization remains central in the fiction that follows socio-cultural rupture after 1848. Chavez's examination of the Hispano's declining traditions and misdirected values is suffused with a sense that a rigid capitalist economy and the encroachment of property-obsessed *extranjeros* underly such decline.

Although "Wake for Don Corsino" is a comic tale about a drunk who startles his neighbors when he abruptly sits up during his own *velorio* (wake), the *cuento* also provides satirical commentary upon the negative effects of American industrialism and an insidious capitalistic system. The railroad, a principle force in the American resettling of the West that has become a metaphor for exploitation in other Chicano fiction, is imaged as having "lately spun its threads of steel across San Miguel County"—sometime after 1870. Don Corsino, moreover, is described as having lost all of his cattle and horses "since he became a daily customer at the saloon, another institution that came with the railroad to Las Vegas and spawned little offshoots in scattered villages like El Piojo." The story has a humorous movement and resolution, but it would be an incomplete reading to seize only upon the humor and the caricaturish behavior in this and other tales when there is a stratum of complex social interactions that not only qualify the humor but give it an ironic marking.

"The Lean Years," one of Chavez's best stories for tracing the sócial commentary that underlies his work, is about José Vera's renewed love for Soledad, his tragically crippled wife. Chavez's tale may be read as a political allegory in which a long self-sufficient village culture is crippled under the weight of time and the invasion of a foreign culture intent upon establishing a new social and economic order. Set in the period after Jean Baptiste Lamy was named Bishop of Santa Fe in 1850, the narrative describes the trip a recently arrived French priest makes to an isolated village to say Mass. Not so much intolerant as condescendingly impatient toward a people he regards as culturally primitive and theologically ignorant, the priest, a figure of Lamy himself, scornfully views a hand-carved santo, a statue of San José, that adorns the village chapel: "It shocked his French sensibilities with its stiff poise, its cheap tin coronet, its staring almond eyes on a narrow yellowish face, and, worst of all, the unreal black beard that was nothing more than a patch of black paint smeared around thin drab lips. It shocked the sugary false baroque ideals in which he had been reared." One need only reflect upon the textual and visual representation of native religious iconography in this very collection to understand Chavez's position on the issue.

As Chavez fully elaborates in *My Penitente Land* and *But Time and Chance: The Story of Padre Martínez of Taos,* it was precisely such a non-native sensibility and patronizing attitude that gave rationale to Lamy's program to de-Mexicanize the Church by displacing, even excommunicating, its native clergy, as well as devaluing those traditional devotional practices in which *santero* art held a central position. Hence, although a clergyman himself, Chavez's resentment of his people's treatment as an "inferior breed of pinto sheep in the Lord's fold" is unrestrained by his collar. In *My Penitente Land* he describes the callous treatment of the native clergy:

> Lamy was chosen on the philistine assumption that French priests, for speaking a language derived from the Latin, were ideally suited for a people who spoke a Latin-derived language of their own. This illogic has prevailed ever since, that a smattering of the language will supply for the grasp of a culture upon its native landscape. . . . The clash which had occurred between the new and the native clergy was due to radical differences in . . . outlook. . . . The resentment grew stronger when [the native clergy] felt themselves regarded and treated as dust by the new broom. Chief among them was the famed Padre Martínez of Taos who, unlike his brethren who either left the ministry or exiled themselves in Mexico, stuck to his post and continued the good fight for his people against all abuses, whether civil or ecclesiastical.[7]

Lamy's "new broom" was so successful at sweeping away the native clergy that not until 1974 was a *nuevo mexicano,* Padre

Robert Sánchez, installed as Archbishop of Sante Fe—after more than a century of ecclesiastical bigotry. Such scholarly knowledge of the Church's abuses and what Chavez calls the French clergy's "insidious feeling of superiority"[8] is embedded in stories like "The Lean Years."

The civil abuses to which Chavez also refers are structured into this and other stories as well. Here, La Cunita is a doomed village. What had once been a self-sufficient farming village is being strangled by the new economic order—the railroad and its commercial effects, a mercantile, a saloon, not to mention a brothel, are imaged as corrosive. Worse, the political changes that have taken place are destroying the villages throughout New Mexico:

> This past year some tall blond man with jowls like
> coxcombs had come with long worded papers from
> Santa Fe, saying that all the prairie around La Cunita
> now belonged to them. The inhabitants of La Cunita
> could no longer graze their cattle and sheep on the
> land. The sheriff of Las Vegas who came with them
> sheepishly said that they were right, and nothing could
> be done about it. After getting a pittance for the plots
> on which their houses stood, the men began taking
> their families to Las Vegas. They found steady work
> right away and began replacing the Chinese coolies in
> the railroad section gangs.

In a single paragraph, densely compressed in historical detail, Chavez delivers a forcefully satiric social critique. Notice the biting humor aimed at the foolish looking *americanos*—flesh hanging from their faces—who read their "long worded papers" to the startled and non-English-speaking villagers. Beneath the humor, of course, is an unmistakable reference to the legal maneuverings of the Santa Fe Ring, a tight network of Anglo lawyers, bankers, merchants, and politicians who manipulated the political and legal system, setting up a land-grabbing apparatus that plundered millions of acres of communal lands. As always, the victims of this complicity between the Anglo *extranjeros* and the Hispanos in power, represented here by the sheriff from Las Vegas (only an instrument himself), were the common villagers who were forced to leave their homelands and slotted into an exploited existence in embryonic cities where, in classic capitalistic fashion, they displaced another oppressed ethnic group—the Chinese.

José Vera himself is forced to move to Las Vegas, a booming railroad town in the late nineteenth century, and once there must trade his woodcarving tools for a blacksmith's hammer and anvil. José, like most of the dispossessed, endures by strength of will, even earns a decent living, but the commodity he makes is no longer his—instead of making furniture by hand, he labors to keep the steam engines moving along the tracks of commerce. Having been removed from the land, such village folk are cut off from their historical lifeways. Traditional social relations are ruptured and people must reconcile themselves to an irrevocably altered history.

III

A final comment on Chavez's readership is important here. I've already alluded to Chavez's early use of playful pseudonyms as a response to a non-Hispanic audience. Now I wish to say more about the author-audience relationship because I believe that like other Hispanic and minority writers of his generation he represents the dilemma of the writer wedged between social compromise and acute political consciousness. The result, I would argue, is a double voice in Chavez's fiction that proceeds from the social, historical, and certain publishing realities that largely determined the discourse available to him when he wrote his fiction. Given this available discourse, one generated by prevalent romantic Anglo images of Southwestern culture as well as by a certain defensive "Spanish" posture on the part of many *nuevo mexicanos,* it is not surprising that Chavez's fiction embodies a rhetoric that some Chicano scholars find politically problematic.

The narrative form that Fray Angelico's social critique assumes, however, was, I believe, mediated by his consciousness of an audience that he fully recognized were primarily Anglo-Americans whose taste for a romanticized Southwest might simultaneously be appeased while also being subtly criticized. Such contradictory aims require a form of narrative camouflage in which a whimsical, romantic, and mystic surface is quietly undermined by social criticism. The narrative strategies he used to achieve such a cautious oppositional form were similar to those many ethnic American writers have used to speak to, or perhaps through, a condescending audience.

Such strategies, unfortunately, have too often been misunderstood by the ethnic writer's own audience, which charges him or her with being socially unconscious or politically acquiescent. Early black writers like Charles W. Chestnutt, Countee Cullen, and Zora Neale Hurston, for instance, were at times mistakenly dismissed by fellow blacks for, in the case of Chestnutt, playing upon common stereotypes of superstitious and indolent Southern blacks in *The Conjure Woman* (1899), in the case of Cullen, appropriating traditional British poetic forms and diction, or in the case of Hurston, offering autobiography (*Dust Tracks on a Road,* 1942) that was racially self-divided. Somewhat the same label of nonconfrontational writing might be applied to, say, Fabiola Cabeza de Baca's *We Fed Them Cactus* or Cleofas Jaramillo's *Shadows of the Past*. However nostalgic, their work described Hispano culture from the perspective of "*nuestra gente*" ("our people") in a way intended to enlighten an Anglo audience.

Fray Angelico Chavez, it must be remembered, shares a historical dilemma with these and other ethnic writers whose work is socially conscious, even revisionary, although it is marked by gestures of social and political accommodation, cultural ambivalence, ideological contradiction. Of course his fiction may be read for its religious concerns, since the stories do revolve around a people's spiritual matrix, but the conflicts that test each character's faith are usually generated by events with clear social implications. However simple his tales may seem, it would be a mistake to regard Fray Angelico Chavez merely as a humble Franciscan priest who wrote wistfully romantic fiction about New Mexico that, as one of his reviewers wrote, portrayed the "quiet lives of its prayerful people."[9] In the end, Chavez says what he can to those readers discerning enough to follow the subversive uses of an allegorical narrative in which historical and social issues constitute a significant underside of fiction.

NOTES

1. In the foreword to his *Selected Poems,* Chavez refers to a personal letter from T. S. Eliot, dated August 7, 1958, in which Eliot wrote: "I have read your poem with much interest and found it a very commendable achievement."

2. December 15, 1957, p. 16.

3. For an excellent and exhaustive listing of Chavez's publications, especially those that have appeared for over forty years in numerous magazines and journals, see Phyllis S. Morales, *Fray Angelico Chavez: A Bibliography of his Published Writings, 1925–1978* (Santa Fe: Lightning Tree Press, 1980).

4. See Juan B. Rael's massive collection of *Cuentos Españoles de Colorado y de Nuevo Méjico* (Stanford: Stanford University Press, 1957) and Griego and Anaya, *Cuentos: Tales From the Hispanic Southwest* (Santa Fe: Museum of New Mexico Press, 1980).

5. Author's Note in *From an Altar Screen* (New York: Farrar, Straus and Cudahy, 1957). This collection was later reprinted under the title *When the Santos Talked* (Santa Fe: William Gannon, 1977).

6. From the cover-leaf notes to *From an Altar Screen,* this comment by Paul Horgan, a widely recognized historian of the Southwest, typifies readings of Chavez's fiction.

7. *My Penitente Land* (Albuquerque: University of New Mexico Press, 1974), pp. 258–59.

8. Remarking on the anti-native prejudices of these men of God, Chavez writes: "It was his [Lamy's] successors, and the continuing flow of priests from France and elsewhere, who now regarded the 'mexicans' as neither morally nor intellectually fit for the priesthood" (ibid., p. 259).

9. P. Albert Duhamel, *New York Times Book Review,* December 15, 1957, p. 16.

The

Short Stories

of

Fray Angelico Chavez

The Angel's New Wings

WHISKERY OLD NABOR BLEW OVER HIS FLOSSY CHIN into the two holes he had finished gouging in the shoulders of a small wooden figure. Into one he stuck a newly whittled wing. It fitted loosely, but that could be fixed later with a sliver or two. He picked the other wing from his lap, pushed it into the second socket, and then stared into his empty hands!

No amount of painful peering under chair and table and bed disclosed the missing angel. The little fireplace of baked adobe in the corner held its single black pine-knot simmering on a heap of scarlet coals. The angel had simply vanished, slipped out of his hand the way sparrows or trout usually do, only much more swiftly.

From days unremembered Nabor Roybal had enjoyed the right of setting up the *nacimiento* in the old adobe church every

time Christmas came to Rio Dormido. Not one living soul in Rio
Dormido could recall when he as a youth had carved each figure
out of pine. There was a smiling little Infant with a slim Mary to
kneel at its side, and a Joseph who leaned drowsily on his staff;
there were over a dozen shepherds in varied, stiff poses, and an
unnumbered herd of sheep—folks said he added a sheep every
year. An ox and an ass were the most true to life, everybody
thought. And above all these hung an angel with outspread,
stubby wings.

After the corn was brought in and husked, and the wheat or
beans threshed by tiny black hoofs in the goat-corral, Nabor
started to look forward to his beloved task. The first snow flurries
creeping over the mesas surrounding the village told him that the
great day drew nearer; and when the Padre wore deep penitential
purple for Mass in the small but massive mud church of the
Twelve Apostles, Nabor knew for sure that the Kingdom of God
was at hand. Then it was high time to open his ancient carved chest
of dovetailed boards where slept his *santos* in a welter of number-
less wooden sheep.

But this year the harvest hustling, followed by a too early
cold wave over the mesas, and also the final straws of old age, had
forced Nabor to keep to his little room, its snug whitewashed
comfort spoiled only by the inseparable aches in the old fellow's
limbs and lungs. He could scarcely drag himself to the church the
first Sunday the Padre put on purple. Christmas Eve found him
unable to move from his little fireplace. Saddest of all, other hands
were to set up the crib, for the first time since the little figures had
been carved.

That afternoon Padre Arsenio sent some boys over to Nabor's house for the old chest with its quaint images. From that
moment the traditions of generations began to be broken in various ways; for the priest had come back shortly afterward with one
of the statues. There was a half-amused, half-pitying look on the
young Padre's lean, dark face.

"Nabor, you must fix the angel for tonight," he had said.
"The girl who was dusting the figures caught the wings with her
rag and—"

The old man took the damaged seraph and squinted at it from

odd angles before speaking. "I always thought the wings were too short anyway. My little Padre, soon I shall carve new ones, bigger and lighter ones."

"And one of the boys broke the burro's left fore-hoof," Padre Arsenio added, stepping astride the threshold. "But that can be hidden by the straw."

Shaking his white, shaggy head Nabor had opened his knife, reached for a piece of firewood and begun whittling. His mind limped back right away to the more even ground of the past, the time when he had shaped these little figures. Before that, as a boy, he had helped his father carve the corbels under the church rafters, and the twisted columns flanking the high reredos. Those days breathed reverence and faith. He recalled how both young and old kept a watch in the church on Christmas Eve before the midnight Mass, his father leading the singing of old Spanish carols. Those ancient traditions were slowly being broken—and now his dear little statues, too. Nabor thought all this aloud as he cut and blew, blew and whittled and scraped on bigger, better wings for the herald angel.

It was already dark when the Padre returned. This time his lean young face was far from amused. "Nabor," he panted, "all the images have been stolen!"

Nabor did not appear shocked by the news. He always looked stunned. After a silent span he asked with seeming calmness, "Who would want to steal them after all these years?"

"There are people in Santa Fé or Taos who buy them for good money, Nabor. Some good-for-nothing in Rio Dormido has run away with them for that purpose."

Nabor did not say anything more, did not even hear what the priest said after that. The Padre left him sitting on his chair by the fire, the two finished wings on his lap, and in one hand the little angel with two holes dug in its shoulders. Slowly, Nabor put in one wing, then the other—and the angel vanished.

A straight icy draught slicing the room's warmth made Nabor turn to the only window. On one of the four misty panes was a dark blotch, like the uneven outline of an angel flying. Nabor stuck his trembling hand through the dark spot, for the glass had been neatly cut out, or burned, or melted away. A few yards away from the window ran a fence of upright cedar posts, set close together like organ-pipes. Between two of these knotty palings was an opening of like shape. Brought into line, the hole in the window-light and the hole in the fence pointed like gunsights to the brightly lit front of the town dancehall.

The old man lost no time in looking for his coat and hat. The smart air outside gripped and shook his palsied frame, but not his purpose. Reeling and bobbing as though he had springs in his neck and under each shapeless shoe, Nabor reached the crowded *portal* of the dancehall.

Unnoticed by the men, who were intently watching two rolling, cursing brawlers on the porch floor, he touched a young fellow's elbow. "Boy," he stammered, "have you seen the angel? He flew straight this way." Had he been asking something more earthy, the youth might have returned his attention to the wrestlers. Instead he stared at Nabor.

"It was the angel of the crib," the old man explained further. "It had new wings, longer than the old ones."

The young man grinned wisely and gestured with a shrug. "Oh, yes, yes; it knocked off my sombrero when it flew into the hall."

Nabor thanked him and went in the doorway, only to be snatched into the swirl of crowded dancers, everybody ignoring him, pushing him and spinning him around from one couple to another. He was in the middle of the long room when the guitars and fiddles stopped, and someone called his name.

"Nabor, are you looking for a partner?"

"No, I am looking for an angel."

"That would be a wonderful partner for a polka or *la raspa,* old man. What sort of angel is she?"

"It is the angel of the crib, and his wings are newer than the old ones."

By this time many of the revelers had gathered around him. "Ah!" rang the voice of a laughing girl. "His wings are newer than the old ones! There he goes—up there!"

All eyes looked up with Nabor's at the rough rafters where a frightened sparrow flitted from one end of the hall to the other.

The music started anew, and the dancers fell to milling around merrily. Once more Nabor was jostled about, until he staggered out of the hall's rear doorway. From across the deep-rutted lane, the brightly lighted windows of the village store shone into his face. A familiar dark outline on the large door pane drew him stumbling over the frost-hardened wheel-tracks.

The dark shape on the door-light turned out to be an eagle, pasted on the glass to advertise some brand of canned food. Inside, Nabor found himself in a maze of streamers trimmed with tinsel. A little Santa Claus, with a cotton beard whiter and longer than his own, seemed to greet him merrily. The fat storekeeper, who was weighing out some sugar with the added pressure of his thumb, called out to ask whether Nabor wanted something in a hurry.

"Did you see an angel fly through here? It was the angel of the crib, and he flew off when I put those new and larger wings on him."

The man behind the scales chuckled as he pulled out a silver dollar. "Friend Nabor, this is the only thing with wings that flies in here, and it flies out much faster."

Nabor shook his whiskers and shuffled outside in time to hear the whistling whirr of strong wings aloft somewhere behind the store. Supporting himself along the crooked adobe wall, he turned the rear corner and all but bumped into the dark shape of a man carrying a sack out of the storekeeper's corncrib. The prowler was about to drop his burden when he recognized the harmless intruder.

"Excuse me, *señor*," said the old man. "I just heard the angel fly behind this house. Did you see him?"

Before slipping away into the shadows, the man pointed mutely up at the dark sky. The silver shape of a startled pigeon wheeled about, like one of those tin lids that boys spin into the air, and came sailing back to the granary.

Nabor would have turned his steps homeward had not his eye caught the same bewitching outline on the goat-corral across the arroyo. Plainly stamped on the door of a shed on one side of the corral was the shape of wings and body, even a halo about the head. But the halo turned out to be only a knot-hole, and the rest a weather-mark on the rough planks.

Nevertheless, Nabor opened the door, which was slightly ajar, and went into the shed. The sharp, heaty scent of goats stung his nostrils as he paused to make sure if he had heard voices. A whisper, distinct in the smelly darkness, came to his ears. "Who can it be?" said a woman's voice; it was the storekeeper's wife, whom Nabor recognized.

"You people in there," he spoke softly, "have you seen an angel?"

A strange silence followed his query until Nabor explained: "It was the angel of the crib. When I fitted him with clean new wings he flew out of my hands."

"Yes, over there on the corner post," whispered the man, whose companion began to giggle. Nabor turned around to see a rooster which had flown up on a post and was cocking a curious head their way.

The goat-corral was the last structure on this side of Rio Dormido, and Nabor would have turned back had he not seen a silver flash on a large yellow pine that had long managed to thrive at the foot of the mesa not far away. Cries like those of a baby floated faintly down from the black needle-clusters. He was sure now that it was the angel—it moved up, down, up, against the lower part of the trunk. As he neared the tree a flock of frightened piñon jays flew away with babylike whimperings. But the angel still clung to the trunk, the way he used to hang upon the crib in the church. For Nabor, stumbling ever closer, the quest was ended.

Suddenly the thing stirred, tore itself backward from the rough bark, and flew with a soft, clapping noise to the mesa in measured downward swoops and upward jerks, like the flight of a flicker or any other kind of woodpecker. But that, too, would naturally be the flight of anything with wings of wood. Besides, did not his ears catch the wooden clapping? The thought put new strength in Nabor's legs as he began to climb toward the bleak rim of the mesa sharply lined against a hazily moonlit sky.

It was not moonlight, however, that lit the higher terrain, Nabor soon found out. As his head rose above the low palisade of tufa boulders, he stood frozen in his tracks to see a little figure hovering a few feet above the tableland. It was bathed in an unearthly glow. Its body was the same age-worn figure in faded colors which he had so often caressed with rough but loving fingers. Its wings were fresh, unpainted firewood, and they moved a little, like those of a soaring hawk, for Nabor had not had time to fasten them tightly with tiny pegs. He could even hear them squeak in their sockets.

And there were shepherds watching, his own little shepherds in stiff poses, with surprised faces, *and keeping the night watches over their flocks*—his own little sheep that sprawled half-hidden all over the dried prairie grass.

And the angel said to them: "Fear not, for this day is born to you a Saviour, Who is Christ the Lord, in the city of David. And this shall be a sign to you. You shall find the Infant wrapped in swaddling clothes, and laid in a manger."

And suddenly there was with the angel a multitude of the heavenly army, being of the same size as the angel but not of wood, *praising God and saying: "Glory to God in the highest, and on earth peace to men of good will."*

With this the sprite-like chorus vanished, and the angel of the crib swept down to the village of adobe with the jerky swoops of a flicker, while the aroused shepherds began to round up their flocks and drive them down the edge of the mesa.

Nabor hurried back to Rio Dormido, past the silent pine and goat-corral, past the now darkened store and dancehall, and into the dimly lit church of the Twelve Apostles. The Padre was already intoning the *Gloria* at the candle-banked altar. Nabor strode shakily between the rows of worshipers, unaware of the knowing glances and smiles which they exchanged among themselves, for his rheumy gaze was fixed on the empty crib far in front near the altar. A flutter of wings among the carved *vigas* and corbels above made everybody look up. The people saw a bewildered sparrow. But Nabor saw a little angel of wood which sailed down to the crib and with a soft click and a clump hooked himself at his wonted place above the crib.

As the old man knelt down, the rear wall of the crib shook somewhat, and through the open gate shuffled an ox over the straw. The animal doubled its forelegs, rolled over on its side, and regarded Nabor with swaying jaws. Then came an old man with a staff leading a limping burro on which rode a pretty maiden. Nabor felt sorry for the donkey, which winced each time its hoofless stump touched the ground. Tenderly Joseph lifted the kneeling woman from the donkey's back; gently he laid her on a pile of straw; and there she lay in quiet, as though she were wholly spent from a long journey, her knees drawn up as she had been carved long ago.

By and by Padre Arsenio sang the *Credo,* and when the choir came to the words, "*Et incarnatus est de Spiritu Sancto ex Maria Virgine,*" the people in the nave knelt down with much noise. Right away Mary woke and raised herself in her kneeling posture on the straw. Now Nabor noticed with wonder that the statue, whose slim waist he had carved with delicate touch while turning tender *Aves* on his tongue, was seemingly great. And whilst his eye wondered, his ear caught a low noise, like the scraping of a knife on a stick. It was Joseph, leaning on his staff, and snoring softly.

The bell of Consecration woke neither Mary from her rapture nor Joseph from his slumber. For a brief spell, when the priest raised aloft the Host, and then the Chalice, Nabor had turned to the altar. As he peered back into the crib he found Mary, now maidenly slim as he had carved her, kneeling beside the manger. Joseph, too, stood staring down over his staff at the little wooden Child that smiled at them from the straw. And immediately the rear wall began to quake as droves of sheep rushed in, as sheep will do, crushing each other in a shouldering pack. They sprawled all about, some even crawling under the manger, as the panting shepherds followed after with expressions of awe and joy.

Later, the bell at the altar tinkled again. Nabor left the crib for the first time with anxious backward glances, and stumbled to the Communion railing, where men, women and children were elbowing each other for a place. Nabor could not hold himself in the meantime from looking back at the nave. At a glance he saw the woman of the goat-corral, drowsily swinging her rosary beads from her fingers; beside her sat her sleepyeyed husband, the fat storekeeper. Behind her were the women and girls who had pushed him around the dancehall floor; of their male companions, some leaned lazily against the walls, others stood idly about the blazing stove.

When Nabor returned and knelt once more before the *nacimiento,* he noticed to his dismay that the shepherds with their flocks were already gone. He had no time to wonder before he heard a faint click. The angel had unhooked itself and had dropped lightly at Joseph's side, whispering something into his ear. Nabor drew closer. "*Arise,*" said the angel, "*and take the Child and His mother, and fly into Egypt; and be there until I shall tell thee. For it will come to pass that Herod will seek the Child to destroy Him.*" Thus saying, the angel flitted back to his hook.

Mary grasped the Child to her breast, and Joseph lifted them both onto the burro's back. Joseph led it out limping under its sweet swaying burden, leaving the gate open behind them. Nabor knelt there overcome by the rise of dismay in his breast, gazing reproachfully at the ox, which glared back at him chewing its cud. At last the beast rolled back to its knees, stood up with an effort, and it too went out with slow, shuffling gait.

The people were all gone when Padre Arsenio came back from the sacristy wrapped in his woolen cloak. He did not see the trembling old man crouched at the crib until he had turned from barring the front doors with a heavy beam and from snuffing out the paraffin candles in their tin sconces along the walls.

"So you had to come to the midnight Mass, Nabor?" the Padre spoke, raising him up from the cold floor. "We missed the adoration of the Child this year. I am very sorry the images were stolen."

Nabor's eyes regarded the Padre's with bewilderment. Perhaps the young cleric was somewhat touched in the head, like the rest of the world. The thought in Father Arsenio's mind was that Nabor was at the end of his days, mentally as well as bodily. Sharing part of his mantle with the stooped, ragged shoulders, he led the old man to his rooms for a sip of hot coffee or wine. As he blew out the last candles by the side door, darkness swallowed up the corbels, the reredos, the empty crib and the lonely angel with its new wings.

The Penitente Thief

I

". . . there were two evildoers led with Him."

THE SAD, MEANINGFUL DAYS OF HOLY WEEK CAME TO San Ramon as usual. On Palm Sunday evening the *penitentes* gathered in the town *cantina,* as their forefathers had done, to go the rounds at the bar for the last time until Holy Saturday. The days between would be taken up with long fasts and watches within the thick-walled *morada* up on the mountain slope. There would be midnight processions of scourging and cross-bearing among the scrub-oaks and cedars and, for a fit ending, the yearly crucifixion on Good Friday noon.

After looking over the line of shaggy heads across the counter, the *cantinero* turned to their leader. "The brotherhood is falling fast, no? Not half so many as other years."

The *hermano mayor* replied with a slow shrug. "*Si*, one-half they leave us when the Archbishop sends letters from Santa Fé."

Shaking his head in sympathy, the saloonkeeper refilled a score of glasses. "*Amigos,* this is on the house. To the faithful twenty—*salud!*"

"Twenty?" said the *hermano mayor*, "Twenty-two, counting Lucero and Maldonado over there!"

But Lucero and Maldonado were not bothering about num-bers. Filling out his ample black suit to the last stitch, Maldonado sat very stiffly at a gambling table, his wide-brimmed beaver ready to drop from his ear, his under chin rolling limp over a silk string-necktie. Across from him and a drained quart bottle peered Lucero's mummy face, swathed in the ragged collar of his sheep-skin and a woolen cap of uncertain hue. The two were beyond waking, the brethren well knew, and so they tramped away to their mountain retreat without them; while the *cantinero,* with the indifference of long practice, dragged them to a small rear room where he cached them among smelly heaps of horse blankets.

It was a strange thing, the friendship of these two. Mal-donado was the town *politico,* very sly and canny as a lawyer, and a fairly successful gambler. Lucero was—just poor Lucero. Their common bond lay in the *hermandad,* which called their attention only when Holy Week came around or when a brother died, and in their drinking spells, which brought them to the nest of horse blankets quite often. Each spree lasted thirty-six hours at the least, very often forty-eight, every single one a span of utter forgetful-ness, except for short but very lively dreams just before waking.

Maldonado always dreamed about snakes and the like. Rat-tlers as thick as logs slithered after him, or scorpions bigger than steers, with red tails poised in the air, chased him over endless plateaus. Lucero's dreams were of a calmer nature, always the same but for the ending; that differed each time. He saw himself as a puny lad living with an old, old aunt in that small *jacal* of cedar and adobe by the arroyo. He saw himself living there alone in his teens, as a youth, and as a man. But at every stage he found himself taking things, such as foodstuffs from the store, money and jewels from ladies' rooms, chickens from farmyards, fruit and green maize from orchards and *milpas*. An outstanding event was the Governor's visit to San Ramon. Governor Wallace, who had just written a novel about the Christ, was shaking hands with the ranchers and townfolk. While holding Lucero's hand, he turned to an aide and remarked that this fellow made a fine model for the Good Thief. It was only later that His Excellency found his gold watch and chain missing.

His best venture, however, was the theft of a rare Navajo *bayeta* blanket from Doña Luisa's porch. It was the size that chiefly drew his eyes to it, and he took it to Santa Fé with the hope of getting some fifteen *pesos*. He got fifty dollars from an *Americano* who, mentally of course, valued it at a much higher price.

Lately the town merchant, Don Jacobo Rosenberg, had opened a bank for the benefit of wealthy ranchers in the county. Lucero was beginning to devise a plan for robbing this bank, when he felt himself rudely shaken and heard a familiar voice in the dark.

"Eh, Maldonado?" he mumbled. "For why do you cut me my dream?"

"*Ay de mi,* Lucero," came the reply in the close gloom. "Would that you had cut mine. It was tarantulas this time, black and hairy, bigger than bison, herds of them chasing me!"

"But, my dear friend, I was just finding a good way of robbing the bank of Don Jacobo—"

"God forbid, Lucero! I have two thousand *pesos* in it. Besides, the government will catch you sure and lock you up in its *calabozo* for twenty years. Listen to me, *amigo mio*. Steal from people, cheat at cards or rob widows, even play dirty politics—but never rob a bank or steal a horse. The government or the vigilantes will get you!"

The sound of their voices brought the saloonkeeper to the door, and the two sat up, shielding their bleary eyes against the lamplight from the barroom.

"Very poor *penitentes* you make," he said jovially. "Here you are sleeping the hours away while the brothers up there take the discipline."

With a start Maldonado rolled to his feet. "Have they already left? *Señor,* how long have they been gone?"

The *cantinero* counted his fingers. "Oh, I would say about four days, four days to the very hour. My friends, this is Thursday evening!"

The startled pair were for hurrying off right away, but on being offered a bite to eat, they realized that they were very hungry and very weak. When they had done gorging themselves with jerked meat, *chile* and *tortillas,* both arose full of zest and eager to join their brethren. Maldonado bought a pint of whiskey "for strength on the journey." Out on the cold street they met groups of *terciarios* and other fraternities, some of whom were former *penitentes,* on their way to the Mission where a nightlong wake was being kept before the Repository. Soon the two friends were out on the steep road leading to the *morada,* and long before it came in sight, the flask had been emptied and flung away.

The *penitentes'* stronghold showed no signs of life, as the only opening in the yard-thick walls was the single, heavily guarded door. All the windows faced a small patio in the center. Arriving at the door, Maldonado asked his companion for the secret signal.

"You hit the door twice with the foot and you say: '*Two evildoers were led with Him!*'"

"Meaning me and you," Maldonado chuckled. Then he stiffened and grabbed Lucero by his sheepskin collar. "Do you hear it? The *pito!*"

Lucero heard it, too, the weird wail of the *penitentes'* flute somewhere on the mountainside. They were late for the Thursday night procession! Each snatched a yucca scourge from the doorpost, seemingly hung there for them, and took the path leading to the Calvario, throwing off their clothes piecemeal and stumbling over the rocks as fast as their numbed feet could carry them. At the first turn they saw a light bobbing among the pines, signaling them to hurry. Quickening their pace they soon caught up with the procession, the sight of which filled them with no small wonder.

For there were only three *penitentes* here, none of whom they had seen before. The flute-player and the one with the lantern were comely youths in very neat overalls. The cross-bearer between them wore a long white gown, and the usual black mask covered his head entirely. The strangers acted as though they had

been expecting them, and the two friends, moved by some unknown power, silently fell in line behind them, their whips singing in the crisp air as they cracked in unison over their bare backs.
Whenever the cross-carrier fell they laid their scourges on him,
according to their ritual, until he arose with the aid of his companions and trudged on till the next fall.

Lucero noticed particularly how much he bled. Shards of slag
on the path shimmered crimson whenever the light of the lantern
fell on his tracks. Most of the time the light was held in front of
him so that he could pick out beds of flint chips or crawling cactus,
in order purposely to step on them. Once, where the trail led over
a smooth granite surface, the streamlets of blood left a design
which reminded Lucero, he knew not why, of that Navajo blanket
he had stolen from Doña Luisa. At last they came to a small cairn
topped by a cross, a *descanso,* or resting-place for the weary cross-
bearer. While the young men removed the heavy *madero* from his
shoulder, Maldonado and Lucero sat down on the pile of stones,
feeling very tired, very sleepy, as though they could sleep through
four more days, maybe five. . . .

And there the brotherhood found them, almost frozen to
death, when they came in procession at midnight. Back in the
morada, they were stripped, laid on tables, and bathed with whiskey inside and out until, toward morning, they opened bewildered eyes. No one believed their story. They were drunk and
were seeing things, said every one of the brethren. Maldonado
himself believed it was all a nightmare, like the scorpions and the
tarantulas. But Lucero was not so sure.

II

". . . one on the right . . . the other on the left."

The following year Holy Week came early, but not so early for
Lucero, who spent most of the time in jail. At the end of one of his
sprees behind the *cantina* he had hatched out a plot for robbing the
Mission of San Ramon. There was in the ancient adobe church a
large chalice which had come with the first settlers and which was
used only on big feasts. It was solid gold, not merely gold-plated,

and of *oro mexicano,* having very little alloy. Rubies and garnets studded the foot and knob and the underside of the cup.

On a spring midnight Lucero broke into the sacristy and made away with this, San Ramon's chief treasure. But he had not reckoned with the Padre's piety. Unknown to his flock, the old priest used to spend the entire night on his knees before the altar, and he easily recognized the prowler's jagged silhouette against the sacristy window. He quietly went to the sheriff's house across the street, and poor Lucero was caught red-handed before he even reached his adobe and cedar *jacal* by the arroyo.

It took all of Maldonado's legal knowledge and political pull to get him out of jail at the end of ten months. Maldonado was very kind about it all. "It was not your fault, Lucero," he had said. "Who would have thought that such an old man spent the night in the church? In the future be more careful. Like myself. Take for an example old Doña Encarnación Lopez. She is supposed to be getting a fat pension from Washington because her husband years ago helped defeat the Confederates at Glorieta. But I am her *abogado*; I get more from it than she does, and no one knows the difference."

"*Ay, amigo,*" Lucero had answeed. "But never let Toribio Lopez, that crazy nephew of hers, find it out. He strikes like the *vibora* as soon as you step on its rattles."

"He is too ignorant to find out, Lucero. As I always say to you, cheat the widow and the orphan, even kill—but do not rob the bank or steal a horse. The government or the vigilantes will surely get you!"

When the *penitentes* rallied at the saloon on Palm Sunday evening, both Lucero and Maldonado were there in mind as well as in body. The *hermano mayor* had seen to it that they stayed sober, for two of the older members had died during the winter and he wanted all the remaining twenty to take part. Even now the two were not allowed more than a small glassful apiece. Once at the *morada,* however, they entered wholeheartedly into the spirit of the brotherhood, hoping to atone the better for their sins the more they crisscrossed their backs with scarlet welts.

Every night there was a penitential procession to the Cal-vario, and then it was that memories of last year throbbed through

Lucero's brain. But he said nothing. He said nothing until Maundy Thursday evening, when one of the men recalled the incident and everybody laughed. Jumping to his feet, Lucero swore warmly by San Ramon and all the blessed saints that it was not a drunkard's dream.

The brethren had seldom seen Lucero angry before. Calling for silence, the *hermano mayor* said to him: "Brother, you have a right to your belief, and so have we to ours. This is Holy Thursday. You and Maldonado are not drunk now, so both of you will go out and see if you can find them."

Maldonado was as loath to go as Lucero was eager, but the earnest begging of the whole *hermandad* at length prevailed. As they were about to leave, the leader asked them if they remembered this year's countersign for use on their return.

"*Si, señor,*" Lucero replied. "Kick each doorpost once and say: '*One on the right, the other on the left!*'"

It had been snowing since noon, and the two friends found themselves walking in a dark and eerie silence that made their footfalls sound as though horses were feeding at their heels. But there was not the faintest hoot of a *pito* nor the least flicker of a light, even when they came to the first turn in the path. Maldonado was for returning at once, but his partner begged him to go as far as the *descanso*.

Suddenly Lucero's heart leaped up, for there by the resting-place, on the very spot where they had left them the year before, stood the three strangers, as if waiting for the two friends to resume their journey. Taking the whips which one of the youths handed to them, they stripped to the waist and fell in line, slowly striking their backs right and left as the *pitero* went playing his flute and his twin swung his lantern before the cross-bearer. When the latter fell, they scourged him; when he arose they brought the disciplines back over their own shoulders and silently followed after. Lucero's eyes were charmed by the amber glow of the lantern which turned patches of snow into gleaming gold, into rich *oro mexicano*; and the blood-stains on the snow sparkled in spots like cut rubies, in others like dark, polished garnets. Somehow, it made him think of the chalice of San Ramon.

At last they reached the Calvario, a flat shelf of ground against a bare side of the mountain. The cross was placed on the snow with its foot next to a deep hole, and the man in white laid himself upon it. While the young men bound his arms, Lucero and Maldanado tied his legs to the beam with thongs which one of the youths had tossed over. It seemed to Lucero that there were holes in the man's feet, but he could not be sure, so encrusted were they with clotted blood and even prickly bits of cactus. Again as if out of nowhere, the youths produced a pair of long leather lariats by which they pulled the cross upright, the two friends holding its foot to the deep snowy socket, into which it sank and was made fast with stones.

All this was done in silence. For a while they stood there, Lucero on the victim's right, Maldonado on his left; and it seemed to the former that those eyes behind the black mask were fixed on himself. At length, at some unspoken sign from the youths which they somehow understood, the two friends started to walk away and were soon running with all their might back to the *morada*.

The brethren were staggered at first at the sight of the two gory, panting figures, but not for long. While both were trying to tell in one voice what had happened to them, a member cried out: "It is all made up! They have whipped themselves to blood and run themselves out of breath to save their faces!" The cry spread like a flame, but was quenched at once by a gesture from their leader.

"*Hermanos*," he addressed them. "Give these men a chance to speak. You, Maldonado, are a man of learning and good sense. Can you prove to us what you are saying, as you would to a jury?"

"*Si, señor.* You can all go over and see for yourselves, for we have crucified him."

Again there was a stir, and again the leader raised his hand. "Brothers, we will all go in procession now instead of at midnight. Leave your disciplines behind; put on your hats and coats and bring your pistols and rifles. This might be a trick of Tom Hutchins and his ranch hands, who do not love our people overmuch. *Vamos!*"

Deep misgivings began to well in the breasts of the two friends when they scanned the path at the *descanso* and found no other footprints than their own. So it was all the way to the Calvario—not a trace of the three strangers, not even the deep furrow plowed by the dragging timber of the cross. When the Calvario itself hove into view, there stood the tall cross, stark against the white flank of the mountain; but the youths were gone, and also the man in the white gown. In fact, there were no other footmarks on the whole clearing except those of Lucero and Maldonado. And the cross was none other than the brotherhood's own *madero.*

That there was something here beyond the natural nobody dared to deny. Two men could not have carried that weighty pine trunk all the way from the *morada* without leaving telltale marks in the snow. Much less could they have raised it unaided, and without ruffling the white carpet roundabout. There was only one explanation, and the word was swiftly passed around until it reached the ears of the two bewildered friends: "*Embrujados*— bewitched!" Someone had laid the evil eye on these two.

If Lucero agreed, he said nothing. Maldonado, however, really believed that he was hexed and begged his fellows to keep it all a secret, according to the rules. On their return to headquarters, all sat around and idly waited for Holy Saturday; even the Good Friday crucifixion was abandoned because no one volunteered to have himself tied to the *madero,* as had been done in other years from time immemorial.

They straggled into the village on Saturday morning just as the mission bells rang out the glad tidings of the risen Lord. Some of them sought the shelter of the saloon, where Maldonado bought a quart of *aguardiente* to wash away, so he whispered into Lucero's ear, the evil spell that had been laid upon them.

III

"Lord, remember me . . ."

When Holy Week came to San Ramon again, there was the traditional gathering in the saloon on Palm Sunday night. But Maldonado and Lucero were not to be seen at the bar or at the gambling table, nor were they among the horse blankets. The *penitentes* said it was too bad, and the *cantinero* regretfully shook his head as he set up their glasses anew.

For several days Lucero had lain in his hut suffering from sharp pains in his stomach. Months before it had begun to rebel against the least drop of liquor, and of late it protested even at the touch of food, so that weakness added to pain had forced the poor fellow to his cot.

Had Doña Luisa not learned of his plight in time, he would have slowly starved to death, for during these days Maldonado happened to be on a solitary spree in his own house. Indeed, Lucero had seen little of his old crony since he was obliged to stop drinking. When Doña Luisa first stepped into the *jacal* one morning, the sick man thought she came to see him about that Navajo blanket. But she did not suspect him at all. So kind and tender was she, so motherly even, that when she offered to bring the doctor at her own expense, he had to own the theft. The good lady melted into tears and forgave him altogether, saying she would not tell a soul. The doctor came later on and gave him some medicines which lessened the pain. He also prescribed milk and thin, un-leavened cakes, not *tortillas* by any means, as his sole diet, and Doña Luisa took it upon herself to furnish all these things.

The only visitor was the *hermano mayor,* who had stopped in on Palm Sunday noon to see if he was going with the brethren. "I wish very much to go," Lucero had told him, "but my legs will not hold me up. Tell the brothers to pray for me. If I get better by Thursday I will go. I want to be there on Thursday. *Señor,* what is the secret password for this year?"

"Knock three times and say: '*Lord, remember me.*'"

The days following were lonely ones, except for the calls made by the doctor or Doña Luisa. Maundy Thursday, however, brought several very significant visitors. The first to call was Maldonado, early in the morning. "Lucero, my dear friend," he said, looking haggard and scared, "I just woke up and they told me you are very sick. You look pale."

"*Ay, amigo mio,*" Lucero answered. "The doctor said yesterday I will not live long. Pretty soon comes the last long sleep, and without your company, Maldonado. No waking from it, and no dreams."

"But are you not afraid to die, Lucero, to be buried among all those dead people in the *campo santo*? Listen to me, Lucero. I had the worst dream this morning, not rattlesnakes or centipedes this time, but a ghost. It was old Doña Encarnación Lopez. She twisted my toes until I woke up yelling with pain!"

Lucero smiled wanly. "It was only a whiskey dream, like the tarantulas. The old lady cannot hurt you for cheating her of her pension. She is dead three months already. She died on New Year's."

"Ay, Lucero, but you do not know the truth. I must tell you that she did not die—I killed her. She grew suspicious and I stopped her breath—"

The approaching footsteps of the next callers stopped Maldonado's confession. Doña Luisa appeared smiling at the door, followed by the stooped figure of the parish priest. Both looked at Maldonado and passed the time of day; then the lady turned to her patient:

"I have brought you another doctor, my son. You know what the *medico* said yesterday. So you will let the Padre prepare you, no?"

Lucero regarded the priest for a while. "What Doña Luisa says must be right. *Señor cura,* it is well."

Doña Luisa grasped the other man's sleeve as he tried to slip away. "Lucero, you ought to ask your friend here to have a word with the Padre, too!"

Maldonado grinned sheepishly. "But I am not dying," he stammered, and stumbled out of the house.

The next visitors did not arrive until late in the evening. Lucero lay awake in the dark wishing that he could be at the *morada,* or rather, on the rocky trail that led to the Calvario. He chided himself for not going, as the night air was unusually warm, even though there was snow all over the ground. Suddenly, a burning pain coursed through his middle and he cried aloud, "Lord, remember me!"

There was a pause after the echo of his cry had died down. Then it was that he heard three distinct knocks at the door. Thinking it was Maldonado, he bade him enter. His heart gave a jerk and seemed to stop when the door opened and let in the light of a lantern. There stood the two handsome youths of whom he had been thinking all day long, and in the amber glow beyond

them was the Penitente in White with his heavy cross. He wore no
mask now. His Face was the most beautiful thing Lucero had ever
seen, and pale though it appeared beneath a thick wreath of thorns.
It made him forget his pain. It made him feel strong again.
Quickly he put on his shoes and clothes, his old sheepskin, his
woolen cap, and once more the strange procession of last year and
the year before went on its way over the snows.

Instead of heading for the *morada,* they took the arroyo bed
toward the Hutchins' ranch, whose corrals skirted one side of the
gully. Several times the Cross-bearer fell, and each time Lucero
offered to shoulder the burden, although from the start he found
that he could not even heave it off the ground. By the time they
reached the Hutchins' fences, the One in White was utterly spent.
Then it was that an idea flashed through Lucero's mind.

"My Lord, You cannot go much further this way," he said.
"What You need is a horse."

A wondering look was the only answer.

"The man who lives here has a beautiful animal. Let me fetch
it for You. I will bring it back tonight."

But those gentle eyes in the dark plainly said, "No."

"Do not fear, Lord; it will not throw You. It is a gentleman's
horse. It is an *alazán,* a sorrel worthy of You."

The thorn-crowned Head moved from side to side, but Lucero had already begun to climb the steep side of the arroyo. The
corral was crowded with mustangs which did not seem to feel his
presence. The doors of the shed gnashed their hinges and creaked
loudly when he opened them, but the sleeping dogs nearby did not
even cock an ear. There was a saddle astride the sorrel's stall, and
this he slid over its back and deftly cinched. In a few minutes he
was leading a very willing steed through the gates and down the
arroyo; but to his great surprise he found his companions gone.
The only signs of their having been there were the blood spots and
the prints of feet and cross on the wet scurf. He noticed that they
led away across the valley, and even thought that he had caught a
glimpse of the lantern's light up on the mesa. As the horse began to
stamp impatiently, Lucero clambered into the saddle, and the
sorrel started off after sniffing at the spoor like a large hound on
the hunt.

Most of the townfolk were in church Good Friday morning when Tom Hutchins stormed about town rounding up a posse of vigilantes to track the horse-thief. Maldonado joined them, for he had gone to see his sick friend early that morning and found him missing. He alone had an inkling as to who the thief might be, and his fears grew apace the farther they rode along the hoof-tracks which ran out in a bee line past the mesa to a stretch of prairie country beyond. Well past midday, they spied a lone rider in the distance slowly approaching the little cluster of hovels that make up the village of La Jara. The posse spurred their mounts and in a short while closed in a prancing ring around the sweated and hoof-sore Hutchins' horse, the half-conscious Lucero clinging to its mane.

La Jara gets its name from the only tree in that neighborhood, a big willow in front of the small adobe chapel. One of its branches makes a half-arch over the old mission cross, and under this branch they drove a team and wagon, which they took from one of the inhabitants for the business on hand. They put Lucero on the wagon, dropped a lasso about his neck, and tied the rope to the limb a few inches above his woolen cap. Slowly the poor fellow began to realize what the men were about. Blinking his galled and red eyes, he looked over his captors. In addition to McBride, who stood beside him on the wagon box, he could make out Goldfeld, Archevéque, Hutchins, Morelli, Toribio Lopez and Maldonado— all in a threatening group, except for his friend, who stood quietly apart to the left of the big cross. To him Lucero stretched out his frozen hands.

"Maldonado, *amigo,* you are a politician and a lawyer. Tell them that I am a dying man who has done no harm."

"I have done my best, Lucero, but they will not listen. They caught you with Hutchins' *alazán,* and that is enough for them. I always warned you, my friend, about stealing horses."

"But I did not steal this horse. I only borrowed it for my Lord Jesus Christ. He was so weak—"

"Say, what kind of excuse is that?" Hutchins spoke up. "Boys, this ain't no sewing bee, it's a necktie party. He stole my sorrel, didn't he? String him up, then, the horse-thief!"

"Lord, remember me!" Lucero cried out hoarsely, turning to the mission cross. At once his bleared eyelids flapped with amazement, for there He was on that cross, He Whom Lucero had been tracking all night long. He was naked now and nailed to the cross, not merely tied. He looked like the crucifix back home in the church of San Ramon, only larger and bloodier.

"Lord, remember me," he pleaded.

Then he heard His Voice for the first time, soft and sweet and solemn: "My son, this day you will be with Me . . ."

The bystanders were so fascinated by Lucero's strange behavior that he thought that they too saw and heard the Lord.

"Lord, forgive these *caballeros*," he cried. "They think that I did steal that horse. And my good friend Maldonado—"

"Your friend Maldonado," said the Crucified, "is a robber of widows. He smothered the Señor Lopez and is not sorry."

Lucero's voice rose beseechingly. "But, Lord Jesus, Maldonado is sorry that he killed old Doña Encarnación!"

Like a flash Toribio Lopez stepped forward with drawn pistol and with a curse fired at Maldonado. At the same instant, the branch overhead shuddered as the team of horses, startled by the report, jerked the wagon away and left Lucero dangling beneath the willow. The horsemen quietly stole away, and the three-o'clock sun came out from behind a cloud and shone down on the bare mission cross, on a man lying face downward at the left, and another hanging from a tree at the right.

Hunchback Madonna

OLD AND CRUMBLING, THE SQUAT-BUILT ADOBE MIS-sion of El Tordo sits in a hollow high up near the snow-capped Truchas. A few clay houses huddle close to it like tawny chicks about a ruffled old hen. On one of the steep slopes, which has the peaks for a background, sleeps the ancient graveyard with all its inhabitants, or what little is left of them. The town itself is quite as lifeless during the winter months, when the few folks that live there move down to warmer levels by the Rio Grande; but when the snows have gone, except for the white crusts on the peaks, they return to herd their sheep and goats, and with them comes a stream of pious pilgrims and curious sightseers which lasts through the spring and summer weather.

They come to see and pray before the stoop-shouldered Virgin, people from as far south as Belen who from some accident or some spinal or heart affliction are shoulder-bent and want to walk straight again. Others, whose faith is not so simple or who have no faith at all, have come from many parts of the country and asked the way to El Tordo, not only to see the curiously painted Madonna in which the natives put so much stock, but to visit a single grave in a corner of the *campo santo* which, they have heard, is covered in spring with a profusion of wild flowers, whereas the other sunken ones are bare altogether, or at the most sprinkled only with sagebrush and tumbleweed. And, of course, they want to hear from the lips of some old inhabitant the history of the town and the church, the painting and the grave, and particularly of Mana Seda.

No one knows, or cares to know, when the village was born. It is more thrilling to say, with the natives, that the first settlers came up from the Santa Clara valley long before the railroad came to New Mexico, when the Indians of Nambé and Taos still used bows and arrows and obsidian clubs; when it took a week to go to Santa Fé, which looked no different from the other northern towns at the time, only somewhat bigger. After the men had allotted the scant farming land among themselves, and each family raised its adobe hut of one or two rooms to begin with, they set to making adobes for a church that would shoulder above their homes as a guardian parent. On a high, untillable slope they marked out, as their God's acre, a plot which was to be surrounded by an adobe wall. It was not long before large pines from the forest nearby had been carved into beams and corbels and hoisted into their places on the thick walls. The women themselves mud-plastered the tall walls outside with their bare hands; within they made them a soft white with a lime mixture applied with the woolly side of sheepskins.

The Padre, whose name the people do not remember, was so pleased with the building, and with the crudely wrought reredos behind the altar, that he promised to get at his own expense a large hand-painted *Nuestra Señora de Guadalupe* to hang in the middle of the *retablo*. But this had to wait until the next traders' ox-drawn caravan left Santa Fé for Chihuahua in Old Mexico and came back again. It would take years, perhaps, if there was no such painting ready and it must be made to order.

With these first settlers of El Tordo had come an old woman who had no relatives in the place they had left. For no apparent reason she had chosen to cast her lot with the emigrants, and they had willingly brought her along in one of their wooden-wheeled *carretas,* had even built her a room in the protective shadow of the new church. For that had been her work before, sweeping the house of God, ringing the Angelus morning, noon and night, adorning the altar with lace cloths and flowers, when there were flowers. She even persuaded the Padre, when the first May came around, to start an ancient custom prevalent in her place of origin: that of having little girls dressed as queens and their maids-in-waiting present bunches of flowers to the Virgin Mary every evening in May. She could not wait for the day when the Guadalupe picture would arrive.

They called her *Mana Seda,* "Sister Silk." Nobody knew why; they had known her by no other name. The women thought she had got it long ago for being always so neat, or maybe because she embroidered so many altar-cloths. But the men said it was because she looked so much like a silk-spinning spider; for she was very much humpbacked—so bent forward that she could look up only sideways and with effort. She always wore black, a black shiny dress and black shawl with long leg-like fringes and, despite her age and deformity, she walked about quite swiftly and noiselessly. "Yes," they said, "like the black widow spider."

Being the cause of the May devotions at El Tordo, she took it upon herself to provide the happy girls with flowers for the purpose. The geraniums which she grew in her window were used up the first day, as also those that other women had tended in their own homes. So she scoured the slopes around the village for wild daisies and Indian paintbrush, usually returning in the late afternoon with a shawlful to spill at the eager children's feet. Toward the end of May she had to push deeper into the forest, whence she came back with her tireless, short-stepped spider-run, her arms and shawl laden with wild iris and cosmos, verbenas and mariposa lilies from the pine shadows.

This she did year after year, even after the little "queens" of former Mays got married and new tots grew up to wear their veils. Mana Seda's one regret was that the image of the Virgin of

Guadalupe had not come, had been lost on the way when the Comanches or Apaches attacked and destroyed the Chihuahua-Santa Fé ox-train.

One year in May (it was two days before the close of the month), when the people were already whispering among themselves that Mana Seda was so old she must die soon, or else last forever, she was seen hurrying into the forest early in the morning, to avail herself of all the daylight possible, for she had to go far into the wooded canyons this time. At the closing services of May there was to be, not one queen, but a number of them with their attendants. Many more flowers were needed for this, and the year had been a bad one for flowers, since little snow had fallen the winter before.

Mana Seda found few blooms in her old haunts, here and there an aster with half of its petals missing or drought-toasted, or a faded columbine fast wilting in the cool but moistureless shade. But she must find enough flowers; otherwise the good heavenly Mother would have a sad and colorless farewell this May. On and on she shuttled in between the trunks of spruce and fir, which grew thicker and taller and closer-set as the canyon grew narrower. Further up she heard the sound of trickling water; surely the purple iris and freckled lily flames would be rioting there, fresh and without number. She was not disappointed, and without pausing to recover her breath, began lustily to snap off the long, luscious stems and lay them on her shawl, spread out on the little meadow. Her haste was prompted by the darkness closing in through the evergreens, now turning blacker and blacker, not with approaching dusk, but with the smoky pall of thunderheads that had swallowed up the patches of blue among the tops of the forest giants.

Far away rose rumblings that grew swiftly louder and nearer. The great trees, which always whispered to her even on quiet, sunny days, began to hiss and whine angrily at the unseen wind that swayed them and swung their arms like maidens unwilling to be kissed or danced with. And then a deafening sound exploded nearby with a blinding bluish light. Others followed, now on the right or on the left, now before or behind, as Mana Seda, who had thrown her flower-weighted mantle on her arched back, started to run—in which direction she knew not, for the rain was slashing down in sheets that blurred the dark boles and boulders all around her.

At last she fell, whimpering prayers to the holy Virgin with a water-filled mouth that choked her. Of a sudden, sunlight began to fall instead between the towering trees, now quiet and dripping with emeralds and sapphires. The storm had passed by, the way spring rains in the Truchas Mountains do, as suddenly as it had come. In a clearing not far ahead, Mana Seda saw a little adobe hut. On its one chimney stood a wisp of smoke, like a white feather. Still clutching her heavy, rain-soaked shawl, she ran to it and knocked at the door, which was opened by an astonished young man with a short, sharp knife in his hand.

"I thought the mountain's bowels where the springs come from had burst," she was telling the youth, who meanwhile stirred a pot of brown beans that hung with a pail of coffee over the flames in the corner fireplace. "But our most holy Lady saved me when I prayed to her, *gracias a Dios.* The lightning and the water stopped, and I saw her flying above me. She had a piece of sky for a veil, and her skirt was like the beautiful red roses at her feet. She showed me your house."

Her host tried to hide his amusement by taking up his work again, a head he had been carving on the end of a small log. She saw that he was no different from the grown boys of El Tordo, dark and somewhat lean-bodied in his plain homespun. All about, against the wall and in niches, could be seen several other images, wooden and gaily colored *bultos,* and more *santos* painted on pieces of wood or hide. Mana Seda guessed that this must be the young stranger's trade, and grew more confident because of it. As she spread out her shawl to dry before the open fire, her load of flowers rolled out soggily on the bare earth floor. Catching his questioning stare, she told him what they were for, and about the church and the people of El Tordo.

"But that makes me think of the apparition of Our Lady of Guadalupe," he said. "Remember how the Indian Juan Diego filled his blanket with roses, as Mary most holy told him to do? And how, when he let down his *tilma* before the Bishop, out fell the roses, and on it was the miraculous picture of the Mother of God?"

Yes, she knew the story well; and she told him about the painting of Guadalupe which the priest of El Tordo had ordered brought from Mexico and which was lost on the way. Perhaps, if the Padre knew of this young man's ability, he would pay him for making one. Did he ever do work for churches? And what was his name?

"My name is Esquipula," he replied. "*Si,* I have done work for the Church. I made the *retablo* of 'San Francisco' for his church in Ranchos de Taos, and also the 'Cristo' for Santa Cruz. The 'Guadalupe' at San Juan, I painted it. I will gladly paint another for your chapel." He stopped all of a sudden, shut his eyes tight, and then quickly leaned toward the bent old figure who was helping herself to some coffee. "Why do you not let me paint one right now—on your shawl!"

She could not answer at first. Such a thing was unheard of. Besides, she had no other *tápalo* to wear. And what would the people back home say when she returned wearing the Virgin on her back? What would She say?

"You can wear the picture turned inside where nobody can see it. Look! You will always have holy Mary with you, hovering over you, hugging your shoulders and your breast! Come," he continued, seeing her ready to yield, "it is too late for you to go back to El Tordo. I will paint it now, and tomorrow I and Mariquita will take you home."

"And who is Mariquita?" she wanted to know.

"Mariquita is my little donkey," was the reply.

Mana Seda's black shawl was duly hung and spread tight against a bare stretch of wall, and Esquipula lost no time in tracing with white chalk the outlines of the smooth wood-print which he held in his left hand as a model. The actual laying of the colors, however, went much slower because of the shawl's rough and unsized texture. Darkness came, and Esquipula lit an oil lamp, which he held in one hand as he applied the pigments with the other. He even declined joining his aged guest at her evening meal of beans and stale *tortillas,* because he was not hungry, he explained, and the picture must be done.

Once in a while the painter would turn from his work to look at Mana Seda, who had become quite talkative, something the people back at El Tordo would have marveled at greatly. She was recounting experiences of her girlhood which, she explained, were more vivid than many things that had happened recently.

Only once did he interrupt her, and that without thinking first. He said, almost too bluntly: "How did you become hunchbacked?"

Mana Seda hesitated, but did not seem to take the question amiss. Patting her shoulder as far as she could reach to her bulging back, she answered: "The woman who was nursing me dropped me on the hard dirt floor when I was a baby, and I grew up like a ball. But I do not remember, of course. My being bent out of shape did not hurt me until the time when other little girls of my age were chosen to be flower-maids in May. When I was older, and other big girls rejoiced at being chosen May queens, I was filled with bitter envy. God forgive me, I even cursed. I at last made up my mind never to go to the May devotions, nor to Mass either. In the place of my birth, the shores of the Rio Grande are made up of wet sand which sucks in every living creature that goes in; I would go there and return no more. But something inside told me the Lord would be most pleased if I helped the other lucky girls with their flowers. That would make me a flower-bearer every day. Esquipula, my son, I have been doing this for seventy-four Mays!"

Mana Seda stopped and reflected in deep silence. The youth who had been painting absent-mindedly and looking at her, now noticed for the first time that he had made the Virgin's shoulders rather stooped, like Mana Seda's, though not quite so much. His first impulse was to run the yellow sun-rays into them and cover up the mistake, but for no reason he decided to let things stand as they were. By and by he put the last touches to his *oeuvre de caprice,* offered the old lady his narrow cot in a corner, and went out to pass the night in Mariquita's humble shed.

The following morning saw a young man leading a grey burrow through the forest, and on the patient animal's back swayed a round black shape, grasping her mantle with one hand while the other held tight to the small wooden saddle. Behind her, their bright heads bobbing from its wide mouth, rode a sack full of

iris and tiger-lilies from the meadow where the storm had caught
Mana Seda the day before. Every once in a while, Esquipula had to
stop the beast and go after some new flower which the rider had
spied from her perch; sometimes she made him climb up a steep
rock for a crannied blossom he would have passed unnoticed.

The sun was going down when they at last trudged into El
Tordo and halted before the church, where the priest stood surrounded by a bevy of inquiring, disappointed girls. He rushed
forth immediately to help Mana Seda off the donkey, while the
children pounced upon the flowers with shouts of glee. Asking
questions and not waiting for answers, he led the stranger and his
still stranger charge into his house, meanwhile giving orders that
the burro be taken to his barn and fed.

Mana Seda dared not sit with the Padre at table and hied
herself to the kitchen for her supper. Young Esquipula, however,
felt very much at ease, answering all his host's questions intel-
ligently, at which the pastor was agreeably surprised, but not quite
so astonished as when he heard for the first time of Mana Seda's
childhood disappointments.

"Young man," he said, hurriedly finishing his meal, "there is
little time to lose. Tonight is the closing of May—and it will be
done, although we are unworthy." Dragging his chair closer to the
youth, he plotted out his plan in excited whispers which fired
Esquipula with an equal enthusiasm.

The last bell was calling the folk of El Tordo in the cool of the
evening. Six queens with their many white-veiled maids stood in a
nervous, noisy line at the church door, a garden of flowers in their
arms. The priest and the stranger stood on guard facing them,
begging them to be quiet, looking anxiously at the people who
streamed past them into the edifice. Mana Seda finally appeared
and tried to slide quietly by, but the Padre barred her way and
pressed a big basket filled with flowers and lighted candles into her
brown, dry hands. At the same time Esquipula took off her black
shawl and dropped over her grey head and hunched form a precious veil of Spanish lace.

In her amazement she could not protest, could not even move
a step, until the Padre urged her on, whispering into her ear that it

was the holy Virgin's express wish. And so Mana Seda led all the queens that evening, slowly and smoothly, not like a black widow now, folks observed, but like one of those little white moths moving over alfalfa fields in the moonlight. It was the happiest moment of her long life. She felt that she must die from pure joy, and many others observing her, thought so too.

She did not die then; for some years afterward, she wore the new black *tápalo* the Padre gave her in exchange for the old one, which Esquipula installed in the *retablo* above the altar. But toward the last she could not gather any more flowers on the slopes, much less in the forest. They buried her in a corner of the *campo santo,* and the following May disks of daisies and bunches of verbenas came up on her grave. It is said they have been doing it ever since, for curious travelers to ask about, while pious pilgrims come to pray before the hunchback Madonna.

A Romeo and Juliet Story
in Early New Mexico

SANTA FE IN 1733 WAS A VERY OLD TOWN ALREADY, A small cluster of low adobe houses around a plaza and the much taller church; but the great mountain behind it lent it considerable impressiveness both winter and summer. Albuquerque was but a quarter of a century old, hence much smaller as to the number of dwellings and the size of the church; in summer it was almost lost among the cottonwoods on the flat riverbank, but the sharp outline of the high range to the east was near enough as to give it character also. Traffic between the two settlements was of the barest, due chiefly to primitive modes of travel over difficult winding trails. Yet both came close together in that year to provide the scenes for a real-life drama having the more pleasant features of Shakespeare's *Romeo and Juliet*—and some of the heart tragedy, too, even if there were no deaths or carnage to mar or prevent a happy ending.

It was the old story of a boy and a girl in love hounded by parental disapproval, the plot found in folkore and written classics all over the world. We owe the New Mexico version, however, not to some professional or amateur purveyor of romances who wished to regale posterity with a delectable scandal, but to a court clerk in Mexico City who sandwiched the incident, as a case in point, between dry and drawn-out legal proceedings regarding ecclesiastical jurisdiction. Other ancient archives from Sevilla, Mexico City, and Santa Fe, help us in identifying the chief persons of the play.

Manuel Armijo and Francisca Baca were the lovers. Their romance was as tender as that of the Veronese young couple, and they were just as handsome and sweet in each other's eyes, no matter how they might have actually looked. The dun adobe walls and rough vigas of Santa Fe and Albuquerque were a far cry from southern Europe's bright-tiled roofs and graceful colonnades, but the great Sangre de Cristo and Sandia ranges made marvelous backdrops nevertheless. The elder Bacas and Armijos, with knives stuck in their sashes under homespun capes, and leering at each other from under low-crowned wide sombreros, were the silken-hosed, sword-wielding gentry of other times and other lands.

Why Francisca Baca's family objected to the match is easy to see and important to know. The girl's parents are singled out first because the Armijos are not recorded as having interfered. It was a matter of family pride among the Bacas who claimed direct descent from a First Conquistador; for Don Antonio Baca, a captain in the local militia, prided himself in being a great-great-grandson of the original Baca, Don Cristóval Baca, who had come to New Mexico in 1600. He furthermore believed himself to be, though mistakenly, a descendant of the already legendary Nuñes Cabeza de Vaca. Antonio's wife, Doña María de Aragón, was relatively a newcomer who had arrived with her parents in 1693 at the time of the Reconquest of New Mexico by Don Diego de Vargas; this lent luster to her own family of the Aragón and Ortiz clan, over and above the important fact that, like the Baca, it passed for pure Spanish, although previously established in the Valley of Mexico for some generations.

The Armijos, on the other hand, were not only late-comers, having arrived fully six months after the glorious retaking of Santa Fe from the Indians by Governor de Vargas, but they very casually admitted that they were mestizos from Zacatecas. Of the four grown sons who had come with their parents, Antonio Durán de Armijo was the only surgeon in "*El Reyno de la Nueva México*" at the time and for many years to come, and was very dexterous with the pen as well as with the scalpel, quite an envious distinction in a crude little world of cattlemen and of part-time militiamen who could not sign their names for the most part. But at the time of this story neither Antonio Armijo nor his brothers José and Marcos had any son of marriageable age by the name of Manuel. At least there is none on record. The fourth brother, however, Vicente Durán de Armijo, had not only one but three sons with the same name: Manuel *el Primero,* Manuel *el Segundo,* and Manuel *el Tercero.* So the odds are three to nothing that Vicente was the father of our hero. The first Manuel had been sent as a boy to Guadalupe del Paso in order to learn a trade as a tailor's apprentice, and there, it appears, he married and established himself. The second Manuel married a Lucero de Godoy girl in Santa Fe (a year after our story), and later moved down to Albuquerque to fill that lower part of the Río Grande valley with Armijos. Then it must be Manuel III who was stirring up the coals of trouble in the exclusive Baca hearth.

But if Don Antonio Baca objected to Armijos in general, he had greater reason for refusing to have Manuel Armijo for his son-in-law. The boy's mother was a María de Apodaca who had been born in a pueblo of an unknown Tewa father and a Spanish or part-Spanish girl who had been captured by the Indians in the Great Rebellion of 1680. Moreover, María's unfortunate mother, after she had been rescued with her child by the conquering De Vargas forces twelve long years later, later married the Governor's Negro drummer. The fact that Manuel Armijo's mother was a Negro's step-child did not better his chances at all. But now to Manuel and Francisca.

In early Spanish civil and church law, when a youth and a maiden fell in love but the latter's family refused to give her hand in marriage, the boy could appeal to the courts and have the girl deposited in a neutral home for some time, where she was supposed to make up her own mind without the interference of relatives on either side. Any such interference brought on the penalty of excommunication on those breaking the law. Manuel Armijo knew his law, at least in this regard, and better than his foes had bargained for. When he appeared before the Lord Vicar and Ecclesiastical Judge to plead his case, he took along two witnesses, an itinerant shoemaker and a farm laborer from the Río Abajo district who happened to be in town. These "friends of Romeo" were to prove invaluable aids in overcoming the many obstacles thrown in Manuel's path by the very court which ought to have been an unbiased arbiter.

Don José de Bustamante y Tagle was the Vicar at this time. As the legal person of the Bishop of Durango twelve hundred miles away, and as a member of the late Governor's family, his sway in Santa Fe was considerable. This priest was an intimate friend of Don Antonio Baca. What is more, two of Don Antonio's brothers had married into the Bustamante social group, and a first cousin of his was the wife of the prominent Captain and merchant, Don Nicolás Ortiz, whose aunt was Don Antonio's mother-in-law. All in all, it was a welter of affinities and consanguinities in higher circles that formed a formidable bastion between poor Manuel Armijo and Francisca Baca. Of necessity an integral part of this barrier, the Vicar could not approve of such a marriage. But here he was confronted by the young swain himself and his two witnesses in due legal form. It may be that he tried to dissuade Armijo from his purpose, or offered him a bribe to leave the north country and join his elder brother at Guadalupe del Paso. That sort of thing has been tried before, and ever shall be. At any rate, Armijo remained resolute, and the Vicar had no other choice than to carry out the law, although with some reservations that were already ticking in his mind.

First, he interviewed Francisca Baca privately, but she proved just as headstrong as her lover. This vain attempt over, he had her solemnly conducted to the home of a certain Don José Reaño y Tagle. There she was to think seriously upon the matter and, after weighing the disadvantages following a marriage with Armijo, return a negative answer. But her reply was still most affirmative when she was questioned some time later. Then the anger of Santa

Fe's society broke loose upon her little head. Her uncles and cousins, not to mention her local aunts, came secretly to the house, despite the threat of excommunication, and tried to dissuade her from marrying Armijo. Her own father threatened to kill her with his own sword. Young blades among her relations were ready to do away with Armijo himself. Even the Vicar, avoiding the church penalty by appearing personally, sent her a message. Even if she were pregnant, it said, everything would be taken care of nicely and quietly. Now was the time for sorely beset Francisca, had she ever read Shakespeare, to lean out the window and cry:

"O Romeo, Romeo! wherefore art thou Romeo?
Deny thy father and refuse thy name."

Crazed finally by these incessant visits and threats which gave her no rest, or, what is more likely, to gain some respite for her tired mind, Francisca bowed at last to her kinfolk's wishes; only then was she taken home from the Reaño residence which to her had become a madhouse. Really, it had not been a "neutral home." Don José Reaño was also a Bustamante on his mother's side. His wife was a Roybal, another family of that closely-knit society; her brother Mateo was already engaged to Francisca's sister Gregoria; she was, moreover, a sister of the Vicar who had preceded Bustamante and who was to succeed him when all this trouble was over. Both Reaño and his wife had given Francisca no rest in the intervals left her by her more immediate relatives. In the end, it all had turned out into a pitched battle between the Spanish-born Bustamantes of the mountains of Santander and a lone youth from the hills of Santa Fe with more Indian than Spanish blood in his lovelorn heart. And Spain had won, apparently, forgetting for the nonce that all her songs and tales give true love the victory in the end.

Back in her father's house, Francisca recanted, to her credit and our admiration. Don Antonio Baca began fuming anew, and this time resorted to a different strategy. He put his daughter on one of his best horses and sent her under armed escort to Albuquerque "twenty-four leagues away," a tremendous distance in those days of travel by horse or ox-drawn *carreta*. She was to be deposited in the home of her aunt, Doña Josefa Baca, who owned a prosperous hacienda at Pajarito.

How often did not Francisca look back during that first day's journey, as the horses trudged down the dusty road towards La Ciénega under a bright July sun, especially when her father's house, and her lover's home, blended in the distance with the ochre earth of which they were made. The last to fade away was the great adobe Parroquia of St. Francis which she had always imagined as the biggest building on earth; she had not been baptized in it since it was not finished until five years after her birth, and she had not been born in Santa Fe anyway, but she had often dreamed of kneeling at its high altar blazing with candles, and her Manuel at her side placing the ring on her finger and pouring the *arras* into her open palms. Only the great blue and green mountain, called the Sierre Madre in those days, remained in sight all day long, seeming to raise herself even higher the further away she rode, as if telling her like a fond mother that she would not forget. But as the horses began picking their painful way down the black volcanic boulders of La Bajada, the Sierra Madre regretfully turned away and out of sight, and the Jémez range appeared in front, all purple in the glory of the crimson sunset behind it; but to Francisca that hue and the rough contour of the ridges were more like the sad purple cloth thrown over the images of saints from Passion Week until Good Friday. It was dark when they reached the pueblo of Santo Domingo; there the party spent the night in the houses of the Alcalde Mayor, the only Spanish home in the entire district. Next morning they started out again along the lush groves of the Río del Norte, a monotonous but easier trip now that familiar landmarks were well out of sight. At noon they stopped to rest at the post of Bernalillo, her parents' hometown where she herself had been born almost twenty-one years before, but she did not remember the place nor many of the vast Baca relationship which came to greet her. The Sandía Mountain, shaped like a mammoth watermelon when viewed from the north, now kept her interest as they rode along its precipitous western flank all afternoon, her eyes scaling each succeeding sky-scratching cliff all the way down the broadening valley, until nightfall found them approaching the ranch of Doña Josefa Baca.

Although Don Antonio Baca knew his sister Josefa well, he had not reckoned with her strong-willed nature, much less with her own views on love problems such as the one he was thrusting upon her. Alone and unmarried, she had developed her inheritance into a prosperous hacienda and had borne and reared six healthy children besides. One can take it for granted that Aunt Josefa quickly won her niece's confidence. She most certainly got a different version of the Santa Fe maneuvers, not only from the girl's lips, but from the Albuquerque men who had gone with Manuel Armijo before the Vicar. What Aunt Josefa did to solve the problem in true playwright fashion may be detected in an unforgettable (yet long-forgotten) incident that took place in the Albuquerque church sometime later.

It was the tenth day of August, in the year 1733, the Feast of the martyr St. Lawrence. This feast day was celebrated by the Spanish population all over New Mexico in memory of those many Franciscans who had been massacred by the Indians on this very day in 1680. While the Bacas and Bustamantes and the rest of the Santa Fe folk were putting on their finery and repairing to the great Parroquia for Mass, the people of the lower valley were flocking to the nearest Mission, those around Albuquerque to the smaller church of San Francisco Xavier (today San Felipe) which faced the Sandía from the plaza by the river.

Doña Josefa Baca came with her children from Parajito accompanied by her niece who drew all eyes to herself—and also whispered comments among the bystanders—for her frustrated romance had become well known by now despite the difficult means of communication. Francisca and her aunt looked particularly devout that morning as both took their places far up in front near the altar. Had the congregation seen their faces during the chanting of the Mass, they might have caught a nervous twitch of apprehension now and then, or a faint smile of anticipation. No sooner was the Mass over than the people began milling and pushing their way out the front door, to watch the play of Moors and Christians and the horse races that were to follow. They had not noticed that the priest had remained at the altar instead of repairing to the sacristy as usual.

Doña Josefa nudged her niece and they both arose and walked

close together towards the open sunlit door. As they reached the front, a young man stepped out from behind the door, grasped the young lady by the arm, and swiftly marched her up to the altar where the Padre was waiting. Soon the church filled up again when word got outside that Manuel Armijo and Francisca Baca were being married. The ceremony went on without interruption, either because everybody was so completely taken by surprise, or because there were no men present of that impious stamp who would dare to profane the holy place with violence.

Fray Pedro Montaño, the Franciscan pastor of Albuquerque who ended this true drama happily without the aid of fatal herbs and potions, later wrote up the case for his Superior so that the latter might present it to the Viceregal Court in the City of Mexico as an illustration of the secular Vicar's abuse of authority. In doing so, the friar makes it appear as though the incident in church was entirely spontaneous and unrehearsed; that, confronted by this unexpected action of the groom, and having questioned the parties concerning the whole matter, he had married them then and there "to avoid greater inconveniences." But through it all shines forth the genius of Doña Josefa, who had previously contacted the friar, the groom, the various witnesses, and who very likely concocted the plot that ended in such a successful coup.

As noted in the beginning, the more pleasant features of *Romeo and Juliet* are here present. That nameless Nurse, whom Shakespeare purposely created in rough contrast to the gentle-spoken protagonists and their highborn families, who minced no words when speaking or spoken to, and who was a most efficient go-between in the lovers' trysts and in arranging for the wedding with old Friar Lawrence, was admirably played by Doña Josefa Baca. Fray Pedro Montaño resembles Shakespeare's famous Franciscan in his human understanding if not in his outlandish way of concluding the affair. *Romeo and Juliet* ends with a churchyard scene strewn with fresh corpses after a bit of sword-play. Although there were no killings after the wedding of Manuel and Francisca, a duel did flare up as the people poured out a second time onto the walled *campo santo* in front of the church. Two individuals by the name of Antonio de Chávez and Antonio Montoya, who had begun disputing as to whether the friar did the right thing or not, suddenly drew out knives from their sashes and began taking each other's measure. The crowd promptly disarmed them, however. Nor do we know who it was that took whose part, for Montoya was married to Francisca's sister Ynés, and Chávez was the husband of her cousin Antonia Baca.

That the Bacas in Santa Fe did not immediately approve of the marriage is shown by the fact that Manuel and Francisca did not have their *velación* (or solemn nuptial blessing with rings, coins, and candle) until two years later, when Francisca's dream came true as she knelt with her one true love before the high altar of the Santa Fe Parroquia. But in the last will and testament which Don Antonio Baca made in 1755, there appears the name of Manuel Armijo among his six sons-in-law. Doña Josefa Baca, too, drew up a will in 1746, in which she asked God's mercy for having been such a great sinner by having, though unwed, the six children who inherited her property in the order named.

The Bell That Sang Again

AFTER PASSING ALONGSIDE THE INDIAN PUEBLO THE
road begins to veer steadily to the left, then eats its way through a
huge shoulder of gravel to draw you into a little valley where
everything is red.

The weather-chiseled mesas to the right and to the left and
straight ahead, the uneven ground and jagged arroyos on either
side of the road, are all a deep rouge. Even the low houses of Santa
Ysabel, their adobe walls molded from the earth about them, seem
like chunks broken off the taller cliffs. The maroon chapel lifts its
rounded shoulders above the dwellings with its windowless
haunches to the roadside.

Not until one goes around to the front entrance does the old
bell come into view. It hangs, to one side of the door, between two
forked cedar posts that frame a delightful picture—a little stream

glistening at the bottom of a slope, where leafy cottonwoods on either bank appear greener than usual, the hue of a rare jade, for having a backdrop of reddish cliffs directly behind.

Rather less bell-shaped than the ones hung in the façade niches of the much older Indian Mission, and though unseen from the nearby road that crosses this out-of-the-way valley, this bell is not entirely unknown. Some years ago an enterprising young priest read the date on it as "1110," proclaiming it as the oldest bell in the New World, very likely a stray from some forgotten minaret in Moorish Spain. Its tone does suggest such a romantic idea, for the mere touch of one's fingernails sets it singing sweetly, belying a legend among the oldest townfolk that once upon a time, when it was new, it refused to sing. The people refer to it as "Zacharías," although there is no name upon it, only the bare date, which a sober reading makes out to be the year 1770.

The village of Santa Ysabel was founded by a Don Remigio, whose last name is forgotten, with a number of poorer families from the overcrowded Rio Grande valley several miles below to the east. The Indians of the Pueblo eagerly gave them the land, as the settlers would serve as a buffer between their town and the marauding Navajos on the west. They even helped the Spanish people build their first homes and also their church, which Don Remigio dedicated in honor of Santa Ysabel, this being the name of his motherless young daughter.

The choice of title was agreeable to all the settlers, even if their leader had not sought their voice in the matter, because they did cherish Ysabel sincerely. Not only was she good, and rather pretty, but she alone among them had a head of hair the color of clean wheatstraw, that rare strain of gold running through some of the Bacas of Belen and a few other New Mexico families.

But no matter how much Don Remigio and his fellow settlers begged the kind Indians for one of their mission bells, bestowed on them a century before by the King of Spain, their friendly neighbors would not part with any of them, not even at a price. So it became a question of making one.

But how? No one in the whole kingdom of New Mexico had seen one made. A man who had been in Santa Fe of late said that there was a new Captain at the Presidio who could do anything, or at least said so. He had already carved a saint for the Indians of Tesuque, or some such Pueblo near the Capital, and with equal skill had repaired some old cannon at the Palace of the Governors. He was a certain Captain Pelayo (no one knows if this was his first name or his last) who had come from the mountains of a place called Oviedo across the sea.

Don Remigio lost no time and had little trouble engaging the services of Captain Pelayo, who arrived at Santa Ysabel one day with a heavy bundle of jagged bronze shards, the relics of broken ordnance pieces of long ago. The red-headed Captain also brought his handsome smile and bearing, and an endless string of stories which he trippingly unraveled in a faultless Spanish that enchanted every one of the village women from the beginning.

Young Ysabel, who was already married, was the one charmed the most. It happened that she had been solemnly betrothed to a youth named Joaquín Amaya before they left their old homes by the Rio Grande. The new church of Santa Ysabel had witnessed the settlement's first wedding, shortly after being roofed, when Joaquín and Ysabel plighted their troth forever at the aged hands of Father Bartolo, the Franciscan Padre who lived at the neighboring Pueblo with his Indians.

And so, Joaquín Amaya was visibly annoyed from the start by the glances which Captain Pelayo cast on Ysabel whenever she and other women, on their way to or from the river with water-jars on their heads, loitered awhile to watch the progress of the primitive foundry which the men were building under the Captain's direction. The young wife unwittingly added fuel to the fire when at table, or after they were in bed, she remarked to Joaquín how clever and gallant the Captain was.

As the work went on, the other men also came to dislike him. Their easygoing natures were irked by his brisk way of ordering them about, but this they would have overlooked since he was a man of arms used to commanding; in doing so, however, he let fall occasional slurs about their own unlettered speech, or about their humble blood which they deemed no less pure than his own. If they persevered in silence, it was because of their single purpose of having a bell in their village.

The day for the casting of the bell arrived at last. Captain

Pelayo had fashioned a clay mold which, tightly packed in sand, lay buried in a hole dug in the hard red ground before the church. Close to it stood the foundry, where the molten bronze stirred, impatient to be poured, while the sweating men took turns at pumping a huge rawhide bellows which kept the charcoal fires burning at white heat.

It was then that the Captain, smiling and bowing to the whole village gathered around, suggested that the ladies drop in their most cherished jewelry. This would give the bell its real sweetness, he said. Precious little gold or silver was known to exist among these poor people, yet several of the women ran home and returned to drop in little crescent earrings, or tiny crosses and medals with their chains. One housewife, known by all to be very poor, dropped an articulated little fish of pure gold that sank like a released minnow into the bubbling pool. Everyone gasped at the sacrifice of an heirloom that had been treasured, for generations surely, in dire poverty. It was the greatest gift of all.

Deeply moved, Ysabel stepped forward, slipped her wedding ring from her finger, and let it fall into the molten metal.

Those who knew about Joaquín Amaya's feelings, and looked towards him at this moment, saw his dark well-formed features become distorted and darker still. Fortunately, his father-in-law happened to be standing near him. Don Remigio's hand pressed hard on Amaya's shoulder, and in this manner the older man walked him away from the crowd into his own house. A frightened Ysabel followed them, alarmed by the thought that she had heedlessly done something that did not look quite right.

Her fond father told her as much, though he understood her motives perfectly. This he began to drive into her husband's sullen head, and for this reason they failed to attend the bell's casting. The metal was poured while Don Remigio was clearing two young hearts of all misunderstanding and casting them into a single sound one again. Joaquín loved his wife too well not to be brought to reason, but the fire within him was not put out altogether. It could not be until that arrogant stranger went back to his garrison and soldiers in Santa Fe. That day could not come soon enough.

Captain Pelayo stayed a few days longer for the metal to cool off completely before the bell could be taken out of its buried cocoon and hung up between the waiting cedar posts by the church door. On that eventful morning, Joaquín and all of the townsmen, who had not spared themselves to see this day, vied with one another in helping to hang the bell. Holding their breath, as everybody else did, they watched the Captain approach the bell with a stout iron rod in his hand. He raised it with a look of concern on his now serious features. Then he gently tapped its virgin lip.

The melodious answer with its humming overtones brought a cry of glee from every throat. Every single inhabitant wanted to make it sing; and the bell sang for every one, quite audibly even for babies in arms who patted it with their little palms. What joy there would be this evening when Father Bartolo came from the Pueblo to bless it, and the new town of Santa Ysabel banqueted in its honor under the stars. The Indian chieftains who were invited to the feast would then learn how much more sonorous was this bell than their old weather-beaten ones, no matter what their royal origin.

Wine, a rarity in the settlement, flowed glitteringly that night along the narrow tables set around the little plaza, which was lit up by the fires of barbecue trenches in its center. Don Remigio had bought several skinsful in Bernalillo for the fiesta. He had also slaughtered a fat steer, while the heads of humbler families had killed some lambs and kids to join it in the flaming pits. There were also roasted ears of green maize from the lowlands down-stream, and shells of broken squashes sprinkled with brown sugar simmering next to the meat. On the tables were heaps of tart wild plums plundered from the thickets by the river. There were great brown loaves of bread that had been baking during the day in the beehive adobe ovens by almost every door.

Old Father Bartolo blessed the bell before the feasting started. The blue haze of fragrant piñon smoke hovering above the bar-becue, and blending at times with the faded blue of his friar's robe, helped to etherealize him in the eyes of his attentive flock as he commended them for their spirit. Though not as eloquent as the Captain, he spoke of wonders close to their hearts, of truths not merely across the sea but beyond the edge of the world and of time, which were wafted back into the center of their lives and their forgotten corner of red earth.

Even his homely puny face looked comely in the flickering light as he spoke about the famed sweet-toned bells of Bethlehem, at the Franciscan convent of the Nativity where he had served as a young priest, adding that they sounded no sweeter than this humble one which their faith and labor had just brought into being. After describing the ancient chapel at Ain-Karim, the town where Santa Ysabel had lived, he assured them that the adobe church they had recently erected to God in her name was no less pleasing to their Saint.

The entire Holy Land spread around them as he compared its countryside with theirs.

The Padre broke the spell to sit down and partake of a choice slice of beef and some wine with Don Remigio, then took his leave on his little grey donkey. For Padre Bartolo would not ride on horseback. And Don Remigio, whose pious gallantry would not allow the Padre to return to the Pueblo unescorted, mounted his readied horse and left with him. Then everybody, except the women serving, sought a place at the tables.

Over the loud talk and laughter could be heard the singing of the new bell, which the young folks gave no rest, and which their elders did not mind. For the sound regaled their ears as did the food and wine their palates, long starved for delicacies, as the mist of piñon-scented smoke of the barbecue pleased their nostrils.

After a while the men of the town, drunk more with the feeling of having brought an unusual undertaking to a happy close, yet not unaided by a heady wine to which they were not used, grew noisier and more sentimental by the minute. They forgot any hurt feelings which Captain Pelayo might have aroused during their long days of heavy toil; they even paraded him around the square on their shoulders, while the women clapped and shouted for a speech in the alluring accents they had not wearied of hearing. Back at his place of honor, the Captain stood up and thanked the absent Don Remigio for the generous pay received from him, then praised every single man for his share in their uncertain venture, for he now admitted with a triumphant smile that this was the first bell he had ever made. The men stood up and drank a toast to his daring genius. Captain Pelayo in turn offered a toast to the women who had fed him so well, and those foremost who had deprived themselves of their few gold and silver heirlooms to which, no doubt, the bell owed its delicate sweet sound.

In raising his cup he bowed gallantly to Ysabel Amaya.

Joaquín Amaya smashed his cup on the table and stood up in a silence that swept down the long tables to the last tinkle of crockery at the far ends.

"My Captain," he started out blackly. "We men of the village worked hard under you, even when you insulted our humble ways and our poor manner of speaking. We did it for the sake of the bell."

With one low murmur the men shifted their feelings around the speaker and glared as one armed camp at the Captain, who now stood bewildered and alone.

Joaquín went on: "But my honor forbids me to forgive your latest insult cast at my marriage bond. *Señor,* if you have any honor, you will follow me."

With this Joaquín straddled off his bench and walked away toward the sloping path leading to the river. The Captain met the stares of the other men, as if counting them. Don Remigio was not there to argue some sense into them, and any excuse or apology on his own part would be taken for cowardice, which as a soldier he could not allow. With a shrug of his shoulders, he walked off after the challenger.

Rooted to her place, Ysabel saw her husband's tan buckskin leggings and breeches disappear in the dim edge of the firelight down the slope, then his white cotton shirt and his black tousled head. The vision was repeated with the scarlet artillery hose and gallooned velvet pants of the Captain, then his white cambric shirt and his chestnut hair. A picture of the sharp knives which both men wore in the front of their sashes came to her next. She stood up with a little whimper, then ran after the two men.

Her scream of terror, when she reached the top of the slope, brought the entire village running after. Down below on a sandy flat next to the stream could be seen two prone white shirts. The men hurried down to find Joaquín with a military dagger completely buried in his throat, while next to him lay the Captain with a hunter's knife pushed deep under his ribs. It must have happened at the very first rush in the dark, the left fist of each not fast enough, or strong enough, for each other's right arm. Their white shirts were fast becoming a glossy dark, but the men feared to remove the weapons, knowing from experience how all the blood would spill out in one fast rush. Without waiting to be told, some young men set off at a gallop to fetch the Padre.

Father Bartolo's slow burro had not plodded further than a mile, with Don Remigio's horse pacing it impatiently, when they were overtaken by the spurred swift ponies. Tightly clutching Don Remigio's middle from behind, the Padre hastened back on horseback and soon had the dying men reconciled to each other and with their Lord.

Don Remigio half-carried his daughter, limp and dazed, back to his house, surrounded by the wailing wives of the village. But as they passed the mute bell in the dimming light of the dying barbecue fires, Ysabel stopped short and stood up stiffly. They all heard the words she slowly and bitingly aimed at the bell, all the more awesome for coming from lips that had never uttered anything so harsh.

"My curse on you—you cause of my sorrow!"

A strange thing happened the next day when they began tolling the bell at the funeral of the two slain men. Instead of singing, it gave out a dull dead sound, like one of the royal bells at the Pueblo which had a crack up and down its side. But, close as they looked and tested, they could find no signs of cracking in the new bell. Therefore, they concluded, it must be the curse of Ysabel on "the cause of her sorrow."

Worse still, when the ungodly sounds reached inside Don Remigio's house, one of the women attending Ysabel rushed out to make the tollers leave off striking the bell, for the noise was driving the girl wild and frantic. Then and there Father Bartolo gravely decreed that the bell must not be rung again until Ysabel recovered from what he termed her disorder of soul. Some of the people were for burying the thing in the pit where it had been born, but Don Remigio's wiser counsels prevailed. A silent bell was better than none at all; for rare was the Spanish chapel that could boast of one, as the Crown had sent bells to the Indian missions only.

For weeks Ysabel sat in a corner of a bedroom in her father's house. Often he came to see her during the day. The old *genízara* woman who kept house for him brought in her meals, which she coaxed her to eat at times. Other women of the village would come and sit by her, to exchange whispered talk among themselves since she ignored them completely. Wise in women's ways, they saw certain signs on her, early but sure, which they relayed to Dom Remigio.

The welfare of a future grandchild, for which he had prayed in happier days, made him all the more anxious about his daughter's disorder of soul, as the Padre had put it on the day of the funeral.

Ysabel, however, was not unaware of what was being done for her. But even when she was hungry, she resented the old woman's dumb efforts at feeding her. She dreaded her father's entrance into the room because the pious phrases ever on his tongue made her very insides rise with bitterness. When Father Bartolo came on a visit, and talked about things she had often heard him utter at Mass, she felt like laughing him to scorn; she even wished to tell him to straighten his eyes, for the old Padre was so wall-eyed that the people used to say that he had one eye on heaven and the other on whatever he could get on earth.

But at night, dark nights when she tossed about on her mattress, to fall asleep at last out of sheer weariness, but never to rest, she felt sorry for the old woman across the room who stayed awake most of the night only for her sake. And the kind wives who left their heavy housework and their children to tender her some comfort, whom she ignored and despised for being such slaves to their daily drudgery, how she yearned to hug and kiss every single one. She sobbed painfully remembering how during the day she had caused her father so much anguish, a man so good that the Lord Himself must respect him the way the village folk did. As for Father Bartolo, she was shocked for having inwardly mocked the saintly old fellow, whose crooked eyes his flock made fun of, true, simply because they sincerely loved him and knew that he did his duty without hope of earthly reward.

Yet, when morning came, it began all over again, that dullness in her eyes and mind, that tightness in her throat and breast, that bitter anger against everything and everyone that must end sometime, or else wring the very life out of her, a thought that bore a perilous hint.

This wretchedness of being all alone, in spite of the efforts of loved ones to enter and share her sorrow, could not be borne much longer.

It was already October, the night Ysabel sat up alarmed in bed, certain that she would not sleep at all. And the morning was so far away. The old woman across the room was snoring away peacefully, for the day had been a heavy one, what with all the corn-husking and the feeding of the hired help. Her father in the next room, she sensed, was just as tired and as soundly asleep.

She dressed in the chill air of the room and stepped into the kitchen. There she removed her father's cape from a peg by the door, threw it over her slight shoulders, and went out into the cold harvest night.

With but a glance at the church and the bell, both well outlined in the moonlight, she took the path leading down toward the river. For a moment she paused to stare blankly at the soft sand along the bank, then stepped across the stream over the outcropping stones, for the water was always low in the fall. Last spring, Joaquín had to wade knee-deep in the swift current while she let out screams of mock fright in his arms. From under the gaunt leafless cottonwoods, bone-white in the silver light, she started up the opposite slope, following a goat-path that led steeply up through a break in the cliff onto the flat top of the mesa, where the dry grama grass shone almost white and the small clumps of juniper looked like dark cattle feeding.

But Ysabel turned right, along the rim of the cliff to a point where it dropped straight down. She had been here before, with Joaquín during strolls both before and after their wedding, even as late as the Sunday afternoon before the bell was cast. How Joaquín had laughed because she was afraid to come near the brink and peer down. If he could only see her now, standing alone and upright at the very verge, looking down at the white beckoning fingers of the cottonwood limbs far below and the thin sheet of water among the stones that reflected the moonlight like a broken mirror.

By spreading out her arms, and the mantle, she would be able to skim down like a hawk, softly and swiftly, and then not feel anything at all . . .

Suddenly she knew that she was not alone.

Someone very near had just touched her. It was like a sweet gentle kick. There it was again, another little kick beneath her heart. A feeling such as she had never felt before flowed up from her fainting knees to her breasts and up along her throat. Slowly she backed away and sank into a natural bench of sandstone blocks that half-tripped her, inviting her, it seemed, to sit down.

"I am not alone any more," she sighed, wonderingly, to herself.

"No, my child, you are not alone," she heard another voice say.

Looking up, but not startled, Ysabel saw an old, old woman seated beside her. She looked like a grand-aunt she remembered as a little girl back in the Rio Grande valley, but her face was youthfully pretty in spite of the many wrinkles. The moon seemed to have gotten brighter, if only to bring out the details of the visitor's features and her plain dress of grey calico, and the black fringed shawl that all the old women of the region wore.

"You are so kind, *señora,* to come," said Ysabel, full of a wonderful trust. "Do you live near here?"

"Yes, dear Ysabel, I have a house down in your village. Your father had it built for me. I come there often. Tonight I came because I heard the child leap in your womb. I once had a child who kicked me for joy when the Mother of my Lord and her unborn Son came to me."

"Then you must be Santa Ysabel!" the young woman cried, not too much surprised to find herself sitting next to St. Elizabeth, the mother of John the Baptist, whose story Father Bartolo had so vividly painted when the church was dedicated, and lately touched upon at the blessing of the bell.

"But you must be cold up here on the mesa with only that thin shawl," she continued. "This my father's cape is thick and warm—and oh, here are his tinderbox and flint in the pocket. I shall make us a little fire."

There were many bits of dry juniper twigs strewn about on the ground nearby, and strips of cast-off bark. With these and bunches of dry grass, she soon had a small fire kindled on the flat rock-cap of the mesa rim where they sat. As the old lady put out her thin hands to warm them, her shawl slipped down to her thin shoulders, baring her finely combed white hair that caught the moonlight like a halo. Then she took out a rag pouch from the depths of her ample skirt, and began pouring some thin flakes of native tobacco on a neatly cut piece of cornhusk. When the cigarette was ready, the young Ysabel drew a burning stick from the fire and helped her light it, and the old Ysabel took a few puffs in silence, just like the old women in the village, shielding the glowing end in the cup of her left palm while she propped up the bent elbow on her right hand.

"I did not know that you were so old," Ysabel spoke at last, snuggling comfortably against her shoulder. "Tell me about your boy. Father Bartolo says that there was no greater man born than he."

"My John was called great even before he was born. I was old, too, when I had him." Here she chuckled. "Zachary, that was my husband, would not believe it at first. He was actually struck dumb. These men . . ."

The old lady did not finish the sentence, pausing to take a few puffs in pensive silence. Finally, she spoke again.

"Well, John grew up and went into the desert, something like this place up here. In fact, all this is very much like the hill-country where we lived, Zachary and I. This is another reason why I love to come here once in a while."

Ysabel recalled that Father Bartolo had likened New Mexico to the Holy Land.

"John's work was to prepare the way of the Lord by calling the people to the baptism of repentence, telling them how the Saviour to come would baptize them with the Holy Ghost and with fire. Later, my poor John was killed."

Ysabel now thought of Joaquín. "And so you lost him."

"Oh, no, my dear child. I gained him. For I was already gone from this red earth."

A question that had bothered Ysabel since they moved here from the Rio Grande now came to her mind. "And why is this earth red?"

"The entire earth is red, my dear, red with blood and pain. It is red with the blood of women when they are not having children, and also when they do have them. And it is red with the blood being shed by men through wars and crimes. Bloody noses when they are children, bloody heads when they are grown. In John's day, the king had taken his brother's wife, and my John reproved him for it, and so his head ended up on a blood-stained platter."

The girl was weeping softly to herself, because of the foolish and needless thing that Joaquín had done, and the Captain, all for the sake of a trifle they called honor, not for God's own right. But she now felt a glowing warmth entering her whole being, for she knew that she had always been faithful to Joaquín. Though she had admired the handsome Captain, not once had she flirted with him, not even in her heart.

"Hearts will ever bleed upon this red earth, my daughter, even the innocent. Why? I myself know it now, but you would not understand if I told you, only darkly . . ."

The old *genízara* in Don Remigio's house had awakened with a start to find Ysabel gone from her bed, and had seen the light on the mesa as soon as she opened the kitchen door. Soon Don Remigio and several men were climbing the rocky goat-path to the crest of the bluff.

They found her sitting upon a large stone, her head and back resting against other square boulders. She was sound asleep, and there was a faint smile on her lips. The little fire was almost out. Tenderly, her father picked her up and carried her back home with a heaviness in his breast that was not relieved until morning, when Ysabel, though weak and suffering from a cold, showed in many ways that she was well again.

Week followed upon week, and one day a man-child gave out

his first lusty cry in the house of Don Remigio. When Father Bartolo came from the Pueblo to baptize the baby, Ysabel told the Padre that his name would be, not Joaquín or Remigio as he suggested, but "*Juan.*" She also asked him to have the bell rung, and at the end of the ceremony, when they struck its sides, the bell sang out again sweet and clear, as it had done the first time and as it has done ever since.

Ysabel, her bed pushed to the window from where she could see the godparents come out of the church and pause by the singing bell, laughed happily and told the good women preparing the christening feast that the bell's name must be Zachary—for did it not belong to Santa Ysabel?

The Fiddler and the Angelito

FROM HIS FATHER FACUNDO HAD INHERITED A CREAKY
old violin and a paunchy female burro, together with a log *jacal,*
plastered with the clay from which adobes are made, and which
sheltered both the heir and the heirlooms.

With these he had also received enough skill to fiddle a few
squeaky tunes and to arrange a cord of neatly-chopped firewood in
the shape of a turkey's spread fan around the low sides and back of
the donkey. With the pardonable pride of a specialist, Facundo
would drive his load to some kitchen door and, having made a
sale, would deftly pull a rip-cord which allowed the wood to roll
gently into two neat piles on the ground.

For years and years Facundo had plied his trade of *leñero,*
chopping and splitting piñon and juniper branches as evenly

matched as matchsticks, then goading his seemingly overladen burro down the steep slopes of the mountain to the housewives in the valley who knew him as an old man when they were girls. His beast of burden, of course, was the same one only in the sense that one generation followed another from the original stock on the maternal side.

The violin, since it consisted of barren dead wood and the dried entrails of sheep, was the very same one his father had used. Like his father before him, Facundo was never known to play it at home, nor would he consent to fiddle at dances, even those given on the eve of the valley's patron saint.

Only when a child died did he take out the instrument from an adze-hewn chest in the corner of his *jacal*.

Incidentally, it was the only occasion, outside of Sundays and fiestas, that the donkey dam got a rest or the leisurely chance to wander off and possibly assure herself of a successor.

Facundo played long and heartily beside the little white coffin at the home. The melodies were the same *seguidillas* played at dances, half-sad and half-joyful as are old Spanish airs, and nobody wondered about this, possibly because disappointment stalks the dance floor and happiness surrounds a child, even a dead one. How the old fellow kept his flowing beard from tangling in the bow or the strings was more a source of wonder to the many children who hovered about undismayed by death. He then accompanied the body, sawing away all the while, from the home to the mission chapel and from the chapel to the *campo santo*, which lay tilted with its broken crosses and half-sunken graves upon the long bare slope between the village and his own mountain slope.

Such a monotonous life, bleak like a surrealist painter's limitless plain with hunched dark figures in the foreground, had to have a break, a highlight—either a bright pink seashell or a figure in unadulterated zinc white, to give finality to that maddeningly endless plain.

So here is one of those tales which change in name and locale with each telling; in truth, the various narrators in widely-scattered parts of New Mexico will say that it happened to a long-dead relative, or that the said relative knew the old woodcutter and fiddler, whose name was Miguel or Juan or Benito, and who had a tiff one day with an angel.

One summer day Facundo (which is the name I give him) was summoned to play for a little boy who had just died. He had expected the call because that very morning the mission bells down in the valley had chimed wildly and long for pure joy.

For New Mexico folks in those hard times long ago had their Faith for undertaker: a child in his innocence, was he not made part of God's singing Court? Indeed, it was only with regard to children that they were certain of salvation. The complex interior workings of adults, God knows, were for no man to judge, no matter how virtuous a person or how wicked. A grown individual was not even sure of himself in this matter, hence the grim necessity that some men felt for bloody penances at the *morada* during Lent; and one had to beg God's mercy on the most sincere and fervent *Penitente* after he was dead.

But for children who died, reaching Heaven was as simple as passing from one room to another. And so they called them *angelitos,* little angels. And no matter how painful, how bitter, a young mother's parting with the life of her life may be, still the church bells must rejoice that there was another being joined with the angels to praise God forever and pray for his own here below.

In this particular valley, besides the joyous ringing of bells observed elsewhere, there was this custom of long standing which Facundo and his fiddle was carrying on. But this time he received the news with a bit of impatience. Howsoever even the tenor of his ways and his calling, the old man had a mind of his own, which balked occasionally, and for no reason that he might have given, just as his burro sometimes chose to halt with its load on a steep mountain trail, or shook off the wood before her master had finished his turkey-fan arrangement. Most likely he had contracted this quirk from the animal, wooden stubbornness being an inborn trait peculiar to the species.

Briefly, Facundo told the messenger to be off, that he had decided to fetch wood from a certain cedar clump that day, and that no dead baby was going to keep him from it.

With more than his usual slow purpose he placed the criblike wooden saddle on the burro's back, cinched it tightly under the somewhat swollen belly, and ended this bit of harnessing by buckling the wide strap which passed loosely around the animal's buttocks under the tail. Then, with the authority of a bearded mahout, he gave the word to proceed.

No sooner were they among the pine trees and beyond sight of the *jacal* than the beast halted dead in her tracks. There was a steep wall of granite on the right side of the narrow path, and on the left a deep arroyo. Facundo stopped to venture a thought, for this donkey had never balked before when not loaded—none of his dynasty of donkeys ever had through the years. When almost buried beneath the fan of faggots, yes; often they halted stubbornly and he was forced to use his stout stick of scruboak without mercy.

He now applied the goad from all angles. Repeatedly the cudgel fell on one side of the rump, then the other. He vainly tried to reach the overlarge bulk of head in front where the great ears were spread meekly outward.

But in his anger Facundo had failed to take note of their position; for in a true orgy of stubbornness those ears either stood up straight like a jackrabbit's, or collapsed stiffly like a pair of scissors against the wooden neck. More blows fell on the end nearest him, accompanied by hoarse threats that echoed through the narrow defile.

Facundo stopped at last; to catch his breath, it is true, and also to find a way of getting past the gray woolly hulk to where the head was attached. For he knew that burros, like more rational creatures, are more amenable to persuasion when the matter is brought before their nose.

At this moment the sound of a thin clear voice gave him a start. He listened, and the ever-soughing pines seemed to hold their breath also.

"You cannot make her go, Facundo," he heard the voice say once more. "I have her tightly by the nose!"

A red cave appeared in the middle of the woodcutter's matted whiskers as his toothless jaw fell. He tried to look over the donkey's head between the massive ears, but it was too far forward. Then he threw his rheumy gaze over either side of the bulging gray flanks, but it was impossible to see around curves.

"You will have to make her back out," said the voice. It was a child's voice.

"Facundo, pull her back off the trail and then go to your house and get your violin!"

Facundo squatted down slowly and peered through the animal's thin legs. Peering back at him stood a beautiful little boy who did not have to bend much in order to look between the forelegs. He still had his little fingers clamped in the burro's nostrils, which as a rule never hung too far off the ground.

His slow mind still unaware of the truth, Facundo began to threaten the boy.

"You ill-reared brat!" he said angrily. "Let go of that nose."

The lad smiled back and did not move.

"If you do not let go of that nose, I will come over and break this stick on your legs," Facundo threatened.

The boy looked at the cliff on one side, then at the gully on the other, and then peeked back beneath the burro with a bigger smile.

"Very well. If you do not let go, I will go and tell your mother."

This time the child's answering smile was absolutely beatific.

"All right, you little *bribón!* Who is your mother?"

"My mother was that woman whose little boy died this morning!"

Slowly it all dawned on Facundo. But when the full truth finally lighted up his brain it was like a sunburst. Still blinded by it, he made the burrow back out of the narrow trail by hauling on the loose strap under her tail, and quite smoothly, for presumably the little lad in white was applying his influence at the front end.

When the donkey turned around on wider ground Facundo did not see the child any more, nor did he expect to. But he did recognize the little face in the white coffin down in the valley as he falteringly rubbed the pine-resin on his bowstrings.

And never again did he miss a child's wake or burial; after that, no one had to be sent to call him from the mountain. The joyous peal of the bells below were summons enough.

The Black Ewe

AFTER PENNING UP THE BLACK EWE IN THE SMALL round palisade of juniper posts behind the low adobe house, old Agapito stacked some hay against the palings; then he filled the hewn-log trough with water from the stream close by. This ewe, which he had raised from a lamb, was most unlike the gray and brownish flocks. The fine wool alone, and the almost jet sheen of it, set her off from thousands of others.

The *patrón* had entrusted this sheep to his care all winter, but now he had ordered Agapito to leave her in the corral at San Blas, so that he might enjoy the sight of her, he said. When the master used the female pronoun, however, Agapito could not help thinking of something else.

San Blas was but a handful of earthen huts by the shallow Rio Puerco where the wives of the sheepherders stayed while their men went out on the range with the flocks shared out to each one. Young or old, most of these women had families to keep them busy day and night; a certain young one, however, had become a byword among the herders when her husband was beyond earshot.

Although the hacienda of the *patrón* was on the great river in the valley, north of the Indian pueblo of Isleta, the master often came to San Blas and stayed a few days each time to oversee the work, so he said; for he seldom went out to the pastures where the sheep were grazing. This time he had called for Agapito and the black ewe, telling him to leave her with him in San Blas. But now, as the old herder was about to leave his sheep for his own range of pastureland, he did not look into the master's eye. Gravely doffing his tattered sombrero, Agapito bowed deeply and trudged off under the hot afternoon sun with a heavy heart.

Not that Agapito had any worries of his own, or about his own, for he had no kin. He was a gaunt gentle fellow with the white beard of a Spanish grandee set on a kindly Indian-like face, and this made it look almost false. Standing among his sheep he looked from afar like a scarecrow in a cottonfield. Nobody remembered where he had come from, for he had not been born in the region. He was by far the best sheepherder on the *patrón's* vast *rancho,* venturing alone deep into the Navajo country where virgin pastures lay, since these wild people did not have many sheep or horses in those days. It was told about that the Navajos never bothered him or his flocks when other herders closer to the valley had to be ever on the watch against a raid.

Nor did his fellow sheepherders envy him in the least, but rather sought his advice about the care of sheep, even if they let his counsels go unheeded whenever idleness or thievery could be covered up by blaming coyotes, the weather, or the Navajos. It was to him that they came in time of sickness, whether it was a lamb or one of their own children. For Agapito held the secret of various herbs, and his hands, they said, had the touch of prayer.

The *patrón,* still handsome and vigorous despite his graying hairs, took it for granted that the flocks Agapito cared for were the fattest and the most fruitful, as they had always been since he could remember, for the old fellow had served his father quite as faithfully. And he did treat him with all due kindness, after his own reserved fashion, just as he now, for example, showed a quiet tender concern for the black ewe.

But to the *patrón*'s wife, who always stayed at the hacienda by the river, Agapito was not merely a sheepherder but a shepherd, clothed with the aura which this word has kept from the gospels and the psalms.

As Agapito followed his close-packed bleating sheep eager to reach their usual feeding grounds, he was thinking of Doña Eduvíges down at the hacienda and felt very sorry for her. A true lamb of the Lord's flock she was, he thought to himself—yes, a white ewe. He was not startled by this comparison that came to his head; his mind could not have formed a more flattering likeness for someone so meek and good. Although her grandparents had been great captains in the conquest of the land, she did not look down on her household servants but regarded them more like cousins. Agapito felt like the father that he never was as she embraced him whenever he came to the hacienda. And though she was past middle age, her dainty hands and her clear blue eyes, the grace she lent to her sweeping skirt and tender bodice, all presented something beautiful to be worshipped.

He would never forget the time when the rattlesnake bit him. While cutting across a field towards the rambling hacienda under the great cottonwoods, he had stepped on what his aging eyes told him was a long–dried cow dropping; the angered coiled viper dug viciously into his foot through the torn rough–hide shoe. As soon as he reached the house, Doña Eduvíges tore off his shoe, and slashing the flesh with a razor over the ugly marks of the fangs, began sucking and spitting out the dark gory ooze until she was satisfied that the color of the blood was as it should be.

It was like the story he had many times heard of her namesake, that great noble lady of bygone days, Saint Hedwigis, washing and kissing the sores on the feet of lepers. This thought did not disturb Agapito in the least, for no one knew better than he that sheepherders' feet are not very clean things. Afterwards, having washed both his feet and bandaged the injured one with cool linen strips over the herbs he took out of his pack, she had put him in bed, in the great white bed where she and the *patrón* slept—for he was at San Blas at the time—and there she kept him for some days until the fever that had set in was finally gone.

All that time, however, he had watched the deep sadness in her blue eyes, and he knew that she knew without saying a word. Indeed, her eyes seemed to say that he also knew and ought to do something about it. But how can a poor *peón* give counsels in such matters to his *patrón*?

It was drawing on to dusk and Agapito was still far away from his usual range, having traveled but a few hours from San Blas. First he drove his sheep into the shelter of a blind canyon, low and shallow, which he had often used before. At its mouth he sat down to munch a piece of dry bread and some jerked meat, then prepared his bed on the soft sand that had drifted into a shallow cave under the low sandstone cliff. But try as he would, he could not fall asleep. The thought of the master at San Blas plagued him like a dull toothache. If he could not admonish the *patrón,* and much less stop his coming to San Blas, he could at least pray for his sake, and Doña Eduvíges' especially.

How long he prayed he did not know, except that the full moon, after coming up like an overripe squash above the far valley where the hacienda lay, rose steadily higher and smaller into the velvet night, its light sharper and more silvery as it dwindled in size. The sharpening moonlight had backed up over the canyon floor, like the imperceptible rise of a flood, until it crept along the outer edge of the little cave.

It was then that Agapito, for all his years, sat bolt upright. Someone was crossing the sandy bottom and coming up the small slope toward his shelter. It was a lone Indian, a tall Navajo.

He had never seen a Navajo so tall. He threw a shadow like that of a long pine tree. He was naked except for a breechclout, as Navajos went about in those times. His chest and limbs, even his cheeks, were streaked with weird jagged lines, luminous in the moonlight. Whether warrior on the warpath or medicineman on a cure, or both, he carried a war club and some scalps on his belt, as also some trinkets of human bone dangling from it. But all this did not amaze Agapito so much as the fact that the warrior or witch doctor was carrying a sheep, a black sheep, across his broad shoulders.

It was the *patrón*'s black ewe. There was no other like it in the whole country; and if there were, Agapito could have picked it out from a whole flock of black ewes.

First, Agapito uttered a greeting in Navajo, for he knew a few phrases of the language. The Indian grunted a courteous but curt reply, and then continued in Spanish, a very smooth Spanish. No Navajo knew more than a few Spanish words, but this witch doctor spoke the language better than Agapito himself, better even than the *patrón* and Doña Eduvíges. His inflections were more like those of the Lord Governor himself, who had stopped at the hacienda with his retinue once when Agapito happened to be there overnight.

Still, this did not keep the old man's eyes from wandering away from the black ewe, which trembled and struggled in stark terror. However, the Indian's two giant fists gripped each pair of legs like a scabbard around a rusted sword. And yet, all this was not half so outlandish as the request the visitor was making in very high Castilian. It was more of a command.

"Agapito, the master wishes you to shear the black ewe tonight, right away. I shall hold it for you and, after you have shorn off the fleece—closely and evenly, mind you!—I shall return both sheep and wool to the master."

His eyes lit up sharply and seemed to spit forth fire when Agapito did not offer to make a move.

"Simpleton!" he hissed fiercely. "Get up before I make you. Here, take these freshly ground shears which I brought along."

The old fellow obeyed as though in a trance. His thoughts moved about freely, however, knocking against each other like panicky wild horses shut inside a small oval corral after a roundup. As he began to clip off the wool while the Indian's massive arms pinned the ewe to the sandy ground, he wondered what this *cacique* was doing all alone in San Blas, and so close to the valley. If he had stolen the black ewe as the prized prey that it was, why did he want it shorn now when the wool was not yet full-grown? But there was no answer to these jumbled questions. The stampede in his mind merely served to raise greater clouds of dust.

Nor could he understand why the ewe bleated and struggled so much. It was not the way of sheep; her alarmed cries were more like those of a frightened nannygoat. What with the poor light of the moon and the animal's spasmodic struggles, not to mention his own poor eyesight and the whirl in his brain, Agapito pinched and cut the pulsating hide several times. The master would be very much displeased.

At last the distasteful task was over. As the shearer got up and stepped back, the Indian's arms and fingers relaxed somewhat. In that instant the ewe broke loose and scampered madly down the silvery sandbed. Promptly, and very gracefully, the Navajo unslung his war club and sent it speeding like a hawk after a low-flying grouse. The heavy stone end caught the ewe in the middle of the back, and she rolled over with a heart-rending cry, like the pained shriek of a woman in the still of night.

The Indian ran down to it, stuck the club back in his belt, slung the limp animal across his neck—all this in one flowing movement—and kept on running like an unburdened antelope in the direction of San Blas. Agapito cupped his gnarled hands and shouted for him to come back for the wool, but the Navajo kept on bounding across the rise and fall of the moonlit landscape, when suddenly a black cloud blanketed the moon, throwing the whole countryside and the enchanted sheepherder into total darkness.

Agapito did not even lie down to sleep. Early at dawn, before the sun slipped out of the horizon where he had watched the moon come up the night before, he was driving his bleating herd back over the yellowish rolling grasslands toward San Blas. In his knapsack rode the balls of black wool which the Indian had left in his haste. If he had any misgivings, they were too vague to chase away the prayers he kept telling on the beads around his neck. But why a dumb animal should be the one to suffer, this bothered him. He would look into the corral as soon as he arrived.

By midmorning he came within sight of San Blas and of the low adobe dwelling where the master was staying. Behind it lay the corral along the little stream. But there was the *patrón* already, and running forward to meet him, an unusual thing for a *patrón* to do, as if he had been watching anxiously and eagerly for his appearance all morning.

"Come into the house right away, old man, my friend," he

said, his handsome face drawn so tightly down as to show the red flesh under his lower eyelids.

"Agapito, something terrible happened to *her* last night!"

Without a word, Agapito unslung his pack and laid it by the door, then stepped inside, his master respectfully holding the door for him and following after. In a corner was a bed, which was a large bison hide stretched across a square frame slung from the ceiling *vigas* by four stout braided thongs. On it lay a moaning young woman covered with a blanket. Her head was wrapped in a towel which she held with both hands.

Her eyes stared with terror from the frame made by her forearms and elbows.

"It is her back," said the *patrón*. "As though it were broken. But she does not remember falling out of bed. I myself did not hear her fall." Here he stopped short, like a child waiting for a scolding, or worse.

Agapito set to work. The woman moaned and shrieked when he and the master slowly turned her face–downward. Modestly, Agapito raised her blouse a little and lowered her skirt a bit at the small of her back. In doing so his deft fingers found the spinal bone that was out of place.

He ordered her to say the Apostles' Creed. It was commonly used as a measure of time in those days, but she also took it as part and parcel of the old sheepherder's curing powers. In a way it was, for, as she was engrossed in reciting the articles of faith correctly, Agapito suddenly pressed heavily with both thumbs and jerked the bone back into place.

The swinging lariat thongs sang out and were drowned at once by the woman's piercing cry of pain and surprise. The towel fell from her head, revealing a close-clipped scalp which was chafed and bruised in several spots. She looked so utterly funny that Agapito might have laughed, had he been a laughing man, or if much more serious thoughts were not beginning to make sense in his muddled head.

Reaching down for the towel she wrapped it around her bare pate in a fluster of deepest shame. The hair on a woman's head is her crowning glory—now they knew what it meant, Agapito and the *patrón,* too. With her thick black tresses this now pitiable creature had been quite a beautiful woman, even to Agapito's disinterested eye. For he had known her since she was born, the child of a Pawnee squaw captured on the bison plains and of the Spanish soldier who had brought her in. Many of these *genízaras* were often prettier and more appealing than the Spanish women.

Muttering something about herbs, Agapito went out to his knapsack by the door. By now he was not surprised to find two long braids and the rest of a woman's hair instead of the much bulkier balls of black wool. Taking out a leather pouch filled with herbs he returned to the room and began making a paste from various dried leaves and roots. This he applied as a poultice on the woman's sore back, and even persuaded her to let him use it as a salve on her ravaged head.

Then the master followed the servant to the round corral at the rear of the house.

There, peacefully browsing, as innocent as any young sheep can be, no matter what the hue of her coat, was the black ewe with all her wool. As both men watched the glint of sun outlining her slow movements with gold, Agapito began to tell his story. When he was finished he looked at the *patrón* straight in the eye.

Doña Eduvíges became a very happy lady although she never heard about what happened at San Blas. The village is no more because this took place a couple of centuries ago, before long periods of drought turned the grasslands into a desert, when the sheepherders abandoned their homes there, and the once shallow Rio Puerco cut through the site to form the wide and deep black arroyo that you see today.

The Ardent Commandant

IF PRETTY DOÑA CASILDA DE BACA Y SOTOMAYOR IS still remembered after some five generations, it is because of the nature of her amorous adventure one winter's night, and not so much the antique landmarks and objects, or the historical personages, connected with it. Yet these other matters cannot be ignored; in fact, they have to clutter up the tale, like so many stakes holding a great tent taut and fast, otherwise the whole story flies off madly into space.

In those days the eastern flank of the Santa Fe Plaza de Armas was a single long wall of rounded adobe pierced here and there with some small windows and doorways. Actually, it was made up of three large old dwellings joined shoulder to shoulder with no inside approaches among them. Each had an enclosed patio, once cheerful with the noises and smells of family life pouring from the four surrounding walls.

[75]

Now the first quadrangle, the one closest to the Palace of the Governors, was a customs house with one room serving as living quarters for Captain Salazar. He was in charge of duties whenever a traders' wagon train arrived from Chihauhua or, less often and against royal law, from New Orleans. The house on the other end was a gloomy store owned by a Canadian whom everyone called "The Frenchman."

In the middle, the house since the Reconquest of a family that had produced no males in the past generation, lived Doña Casilda in a solitary splendor not evident from without.

For she had inherited not only her father's house and the heirlooms of the past hundred years, since the Reconquistador De Vargas had laid out anew the Plaza de Armas and assigned the choicest lots fronting it to favorite captains, but she owned five well–stocked *ranchos* left her by her father, her mother, and her three husbands.

Doña Casilda still had many years to enjoy all her wealth, since she was not quite forty. But she was not enjoying it, alone as she was and lonely, even though her many friends often came to loll through an afternoon's chocolate *merienda* among the furnishings in her living room that they never ceased to covet and admire.

Her only door and window on the Plaza belonged to this room. It ran back like a long salon, where a larger window quaffed in the light from the patio at the far end, so that the thick and uneven whitewashed walls and the coffee–hued ceiling *vigas* were neither buried in cold gloom nor lighted so much as to betray their old primitive crudeness. With a large fireplace and an ancient crucifix above it at the far corner, a rich French tapestry against the end wall, smaller oil canvases of saints in goldleaf frames along the side walls, and many polished brass candelabra standing on hand–carved chests and tables on either side, it looked to be part chapel and part drawing-room at first glance. But strewn all over the uneven floor lay thick Indian blankets, most a rich red, which lent so much warmth that the chapel idea gave way to that of a medieval royal drawing–room.

A queen's chamber, her friends called it, although they had never seen a queen or a castle. And, said they to themselves, it was too bad that there was no king. Only a royal consort was missing, but they went no further along this trend of thought.

Next to the front entrance a deep doorway through the thick adobe wall led to her bedroom. Her large bed by the front wall stood almost lost in shadow. Its outline and a flower-embroidered bedspread appeared faintly because a fat candle, set in a flat dish on a bracket above the bedstead, lit up a small painting of Our Lady of Light.

It was a charming miniature, finely painted over a sheet of copper, of the large central painting on the great stone reredos at the military chapel. The Lord Bishop had given it to her, the same day he consecrated the new military chapel with its wonderful reredos and the beautiful painting of Our Lady of Light enthroned in its center. Casilda was not quite seven years old then, but she remembered. No bishop from Durango had visited Santa Fe since, but she remembered how he looked and how he was dressed, because his Lordship held her on his knee and told her she was a very pretty angel. It was then that he gave her the miniature, to protect her all her life, his Lordship said, just as Mary with her Child in the painting was snatching a youth away from the jagged jaws of a fierce dragon.

And a light had burned before that little painting ever since, day and night, even after she was married—three times—when her husbands were home and also when they went away, and ever since, night and day. . . .

From the bedroom another door led into a dim diningroom, but seldom used, and from here flanking the patio followed the kitchen and other rooms, Juana's bedroom among them. Juana was an Indian girl who cooked the meals and took care of the entire house. She had been brought as a little child by Casilda's first husband when he returned from a Ute campaign, the one before the Apache battle when he was killed. Juana was a very good cook, and she took great delight in rubbing the many brass chandeliers and single candlesticks until they shone like gold. She loved Casilda like a mother and served her like a queen. Whenever they went to church, or visiting, Juana walked ahead. When going to the chapel she carried a folded blanket which she spread on the dirt floor for her mistress to kneel on during Mass, and to squat on during the sermon.

On such occasions, when not busy with the honor guard of the Palace, Captain Salazar gallantly escorted her. He was her first cousin and more like a brother, for he and Casilda had been reared together as children. He went in and out of the house as though it were his own, and no one thought evil of it because he was a good man. When soldiers say this of an officer they know well it must be true. In fact, people had thought that she should have married him, after her second husband died and she married her third. There were good reasons for the Vicar's granting a dispensation, since available younger men of her station were scarce, and she had been widowed thrice by war while he had recently lost his wife in childbirth. The captain had not married again, and it was a pity that he could not be Casilda's fourth husband.

Another but less frequent visitor was the Frenchman. He was attracted by the large store of old French and Spanish wines in a dark room off the kitchen. Her father and grandfather had for years bought the contraband Burgundy from New Orleans; the legal Spanish wines had come in casks from Jerez to Mexico City, and some bottles of it had made their way up to Santa Fe. In turn, Casilda was rewarded by the tales the Frenchman told about far Quebec and New Orleans. He had also been to Paris. Many took this foreign merchant for a spy. It was whispered about that he kept an evergrowing cache of lead ingots and kegs of gunpowder, against the day when French colonial troops from Louisiana invaded New Mexico. This gave birth to a rumor that Casilda was lending her dark storerooms to his nefarious schemes.

Captain Salazar, more than half believing the gossip, had asked Casilda if it were true, and she had angrily told him to search the entire house if he wished. Since then the Captain had not come to see her, and she had told the Frenchman to stay away.

Now she was lonelier than ever.

One cold evening in late March, Casilda sat waiting anxiously at her front window, where she often passed long hours, for the small opening provided a clear view of the treeless Plaza, where everything worthwhile knowing in Santa Fe happened, or was reported. To learn further details she sometimes sent Juana to find out. Today the new Lord Governor was to have arrived with his entourage, but the Plaza was also bare of people, save for squads of soldiers drilling in front of the Palace. Captain Salazar was setting the men through their paces.

Although her room was comfortably warm because of the droning fireplace in the far corner, Casilda shivered for the poor men in uniform out in the cold. It was so cold that none of the usual loiterers was in sight anywhere. The western sky was orange and yellow, like her fireplace behind her, and the sunset touched with flaming light the lengthy log-pillared porch of the Palace to her right and the tall adobe parapet of the military chapel opposite, to her left. But it was a cold light, frozen by the air sweeping down from the high sierra behind her house and the parish church and the eastern reaches of the town.

Besides, she missed the captain's company.

"Juana," she called out to her girl in the kitchen. "Juana, go out and ask my cousin why the Lord Governor did not come today. And be sure to put on a blanket. The soldiers look frozen from here."

The Ute maiden went out leaning against the unseen wind and promptly started back with Captain Salazar, who had been dismissing the guard when the servant spoke to him.

"God give you a good evening, *prima*," he said blusteringly when he came in the door, as though no angry words had ever passed between them. Making for the fireplace, he turned around with his back to the flames, and began rocking in his boots to limber his toes.

"The Lord Governor and his party got bogged down at La Cienega early this afternoon. His carriage and the freight carts sank down in the mud, a runner just told me. By now the wheels ought to be gripped tight by the icy swamp."

"So there will be no reception today?"

"It would be foolish, dear cousin. Tonight his Excellency and his Lady arrive together with his staff. They are on their way from La Cienega on horseback. We will let them rest well tonight, and late tomorrow morning until the sun is well up and the air warm. Then, at ten or eleven, we escort them to the Mass of Reception at Our Lady of Light. Father Hocio thinks this plan most excellent. In the evening—you know, the ball at the Palace. May I escort you to it, Casilda?"

"Who else would? The Frenchman?" She laughed girlishly, and then invited her now thawed-out cousin to stay for supper.

The next day, from her window, Doña Casilda watched the

parade from the Palace porch straight across the Plaza to the military chapel of Our Lady of Light. From early morning the square had begun to teem with people of every description, inhabitants of the Capital and folks from the *ranchos* who had come in the day before, and also many Indians from nearby Tesuque. Casilda's landowning lady friends from town and from the country arrived with their husbands shortly before the procession began. It was a short one, of course, and as soon as the Lord Governor and his retinue disappeared into the wide doorway of the military chapel, followed by the leading officials and citizens of the region, Casilda called Juana and they started forth in single file.

Casilda wore her best dress of black silk with a black wool shawl over her shoulders. The smooth fair skin of her face, and the bloom on her cheeks brought on by the chill air, were further livened by a scarlet geranium pinned over her black lace mantilla, just above her left temple. Juana tended these flowers for this one use.

Captain Salazar saw them coming and ordered the guard to attention as Casilda sauntered between the two lines of soldiers at the church door. She bowed and smiled, and the men grinned behind their raised muskets, which they would not have dared do when his Excellency went by.

With Juana opening a path for her through the dark crowded nave, Casilda pushed toward the sunlight-bathed reredos and soon reached her accustomed place far in front to the right, almost beneath the pulpit of carved stone. She promptly knelt down on the blanket which her girl had spread out on the floor.

The Lord Governor was already seated at his red-canopied throne in the transept to her left, and next to him on a chair below the platform sat his Lady. She appeared to be a very kindly woman. Casilda would find out tonight at the reception. Seated around were the Mayor and his Council, all of whom she knew well. They were all her relatives.

But standing about on either side of the throne were several strangers in the latest style of uniforms, breathtaking in their gold-braided chests and high open collars, their epaulets shimmering on wide shoulders. Their tallness and younger years obscured his

Excellency in all his panoply of solid gold embroidery and bright ribbands. They were his personal staff from the City of Mexico. She tried to guess who were single and who were married, or at least widowers, when a bell in the sacristy tinkled and out came three Padres vested for a Solemn High Mass.

The celebrant was Father Hocio, the military chaplain of the Presidio and Our Lady of Light, assisted by two other Franciscans from the parish church of San Francisco up the street. Father Hocio, leaving his deacons seated by the reredos, went up the pulpit to read the royal proclamation and say some words of welcome to the Lord Governor. He did it very calmly, as if little awed by officialdom, and looked quite imposing himself, and much younger than his years, in those beautiful pearl-hued vestments. Everyone knew that he had spent long hard years in the most difficult missions, and had stared into the face of death many times as chaplain to the colonial troops. Casilda knew this well. It was he who had anointed and comforted each of her three husbands in their final hour. It was he, too, who had allayed and soothed her despairing grief, each of those three times. She trusted him with all her thoughts, and he sometimes confided in her.

If only the Crown sent new muskets to equip the militia, he had often said to her, instead of new suits for the Lord Governor's honor guard every other year, the colonial troops would not have to defend the region with fire-sharpened oakpoles for lances, and thus leave so many widows and orphans.

"Casilda, you ought to get married again," he had said to her in the sacristy, one afternoon when she had consulted him there. "You are still young and attractive, my daughter, and a lady of lineage and means. Oh, yes, I know all about that crazy superstition among your people, that no one may marry a fourth time. It is all foolishness, all plain foolishness."

New Mexico was full of males who had married three times, and there were many women who had had three husbands. In a harsh and isolated land without doctors, many a young wife died in childbirth or in one of many recurring epidemics. Surrounded as the country was by marauding Indians of every tribe, many with good firearms bought from the French along the Mississippi, scores of New Mexico husbands died in the frequent campaigns, or else were ambushed and scalped while rounding up their sheep or cattle. Usually, by the time the third marriage ended through a natural death, if not an Indian massacre, the surviving party was too old and tired to want, or attract, a fourth mating.

And so the unspoken belief had grown that a fourth marriage was either viewed askance by God or awaited with glee by mischievous evil spirits.

But Casilda had lost her men young, within the year after each marriage, all killed in a skirmish or an ambuscade. Unlike other widows, most of them poor, she had borne no children; two unborn ones had each been killed by the shocking news of violent death. This is why she always helped certain orphans in Santa Fe, but this did not fill an invisible hollow that kept on yearning for highpitched voices and laughter among her carved chests and polished candlesticks and in her deserted patio. Perhaps this was why she never raised her voice in anger at Juana, the Ute captive whom she had reared like her own baby.

Father Hocio and his attending ministers began the Mass at the foot of the altar—after the Lord Governor had been properly welcomed and installed. Casilda set her mind at prayerful attention, as she had learned to do since she was a little girl, ever since the bishop came and blessed the new chapel and its beautiful altar, since the day her father and mother beamed with pride when his Lordship visited their house and held her on his knee, and she got that little painting of Our Lady of Light that still hung above her bed with a lit candle before it.

She did this by first contemplating the carven bas-reliefs on the lofty stone reredos, which now loomed up mysteriously through the incense smoke that climbed up ladders of sunlight to the clerestory above.

Starting down from the rounded peak of the reredos, where the Eternal Father in his triple tiara blessed everything below, Casilda prayed for her father.

Beneath was the Madonna and Child, Our Lady of Valvanera, seated in the hollow of an ancient oak in her forest shrine in Navarre across the seas. To her she commended the saintly soul of her mother.

Below this was the panel of Santiago the Apostle, who converted Spain; he was on horseback striving with raised sword for the Spanish armies against the Moors. In panels on either side of him were San José, patron of a happy death because he died in the arms of Jesus, and San Juan Nepomuceno holding his martyr's palm. To these three she had learned with the tragic years to entrust the souls of her three martyred soldier-husbands—and strange that their names should have been Santiago, José, and Juan . . .

But to Casilda the most beautiful of all was the large oil painting of *Nuestra Señora de la Luz,* enthroned in the center of the reredos, just above the head of Father Hocio. Our Lady of Light wore a white gown and flowing blue mantle, holding her Infant on her left arm, and with the other hand rescuing a young man from the gaping maw of an infernal monster. The Holy Child smilingly directed the operation. But it seemed to Casilda that the youth being helped didn't seem to care much whether he was saved or not. The artist had given him a blank look. Maybe he was stupid about such things, like so many people.

Anyway, the figures and colors were richly distracting. They were exactly like those in the miniature above her bed, as though that picture had been stretched out by magic to become this one on the altar, or the other way around. In fact, Casilda could do the trick at will by squinting hard . . .

By now she no longer heard Father Hocio's Latin chant, nor the shuffling and the coughing of the crowds behind her. Glancing toward the left transept, without daring to turn her head, she could plainly see a certain officer next to the Lord Governor. He was a tall Commandant, with a sharp widow's peak on his high forehead. Was he married? Such a man, surely, would not be afraid of a local superstition. From his self-assured stance, Casilda guessed, he must have been all over the world. Perhaps he was from the Court of Madrid. The thought thrilled her, for a Spaniard from Europe was a greater prize than a Creole from New Spain.

Once, for the space of a wink, Casilda was sure he had looked meaningly at her.

She would meet him at the ball tonight, and he might ask for an assignation. Still, was it not wrong to admit a stranger into one's home, and at such a late hour? What if he proposed something sinful? Officers who came to Santa Fe from the outside world were usually very bold in this regard. And Father Hocio had often preached about the dangers of becoming entangled; the near occasion of sin was more wily than the sudden bare face of evil. And yet, the Padre himself had told her that she ought to get married.

Suppose the Commandant did ask to take her home after the reception, and she declined—would he want to see her again? She was not too young any more. Under the circumstances she had a good reason to say "yes."

Sometime later, Casilda felt Juana's hand shoving something into hers under the shawl. It was a folded bit of paper. Juana whispered that she did not know who had given it to her. It must have been some other servant in the packed throng behind them. She opened the tiny sheet flat and was struck right away by the handsome script. Her full name lay traced in delicate scrolls. It was not the uneven halting handwriting of folks in Santa Fe who could write. Slowly, and with a rising thrill, she read the message:

> *"Not until now have I seen such a rose in full bloom, such a rare apple in full ripeness, I who have seen the best gardens and groves of the whole world. Do forgive this my heart for being overbold, my dear Lady, but it is gone mad with your beauty. May I visit with you alone tonight, after the reception at the Palace? If you accept, which you must, will you give me this sign? As you leave the chapel this morning, do not take holy water at the font. I will be watching. Kissing your hand, I am your unworthy servant and slave,*
>
> *Commandante del Fuego."*

Commandante del Fuego! Nobility! Perhaps the land called Tierra del Fuego was named after a great Conquistador who was his grandfather. And he himself must be the new commander of the Presidio.

It had to be the tall officer with the handsome widow's peak. Tempted to look over, she checked herself. He must surely be staring at her right now. She must give no sign of her excitment, even though she must look quite flustered already.

He looked handsomer still as he left the church with the others in the Governor's retinue. Nudging her girl, Casilda followed Juana after the crowds that were elbowing their way out into the sunlit square. Juana took holy water from the carved stone font and crossed herself as she went out the door. Casilda reached out by force of habit, paused for a moment, and then brought her hand back under the shawl on her arm, where she still held the folded bit of paper in a trembling clenched fist.

It was like a dream, the way she and Juana skirted around the rear of the milling throngs on the Plaza, still cheering the Lord Governor as he vanished into the Palace. They reached home unnoticed, and Casilda began ordering the girl to sweep and dust the entire house and polish the brass candelabra, although she had done all this yesterday.

The evening arrived in a hurry. Shortly before eight, Casilda received word from Captain Salazar that he could not come for her. So much the better, she thought.

When the time came, Juana led her across the short corner-space of Plaza to the main entrance of the Palace of the Governors. The long parapet of its *portal,* and the whole Plaza in front, were already powdered white with the first flakes of a snowfall that promised to flutter down all night. While she loved snow, to watch through the window from her cozy room, tonight she enjoyed walking on it. It reminded her of clouds, and her feet treading on them far above the real world.

As Juana hied herself to the servants' quarters beyond the wide *zaguán,* Casilda went into the Palace ballroom to make her own grand entrance. Some of her friends and relations came forward to greet her and then presented her to the Lord Governor and his Lady. Her Ladyship at close ranged proved to be what she had appeared in church. But soon Casilda was away with the new officers, all most charming in their manner and address. All of them took turns in dancing with her whenever the musicians struck up a *seguidilla.*

But none of them was named "del Fuego." And she dared not ask. Perhaps one of these strangers had played a prank on her to amuse his companions, for these court people from the Viceregal Capital of New Spain felt themselves much superior to the best in the provinces. She must not give them the chance of enjoying the success of their prank.

She also looked in vain for Captain Salazar. He must have been called away on something really important and serious, to miss this reception even when he had been unable to escort her to it. Harried by her suspicions, Casilda excused herself well before midnight and joined her girl in the hallway, where Juana had been waiting for some time.

Outside, the snow had risen to the height of a man's hand, and the swirling flakes were coming down thicker than before. As Juana plunged ahead into the white world, the strong hand of a man reached out from the shadows of the *portal* and took Casilda's shoulder. She turned to see a tall military figure in a great dark cape half-hidden by the black shade of a wooden pillar. But there was enough light from a window to bring out his handsome features at the moment, and a bit of the widow's peak.

"I am the Commandante del Fuego," he said. "I could not come to the ball because one of my men shot himself tonight, and I could not leave him until—Casilda, may I still come?"

"But of course," she stammered quickly.

He was indeed far more handsome, and taller, than the other staff officers she had danced with tonight, Casilda thought breathlessly as she caught up silently behind Juana, who had not felt her absence for the moment. And how tender and considerate the Commandant must be, if he missed the reception to stay by the side of a common soldier in his last need.

After she had revived the flames in the corner fireplace, and brought out two bottles of the Burgundy and the Jerez, which the Frenchman said were of the best, she touched a long sliver of pine to the fire and glided with it from candle to candle all around the room until it glittered like a palace in dreams.

She had barely fastened the shutters of her window when a soft knock at the door made her reach it quickly to pull back the bolt. Hastily shaking the snow off his mantle, and off his pointed admiralty hat that had an ostrich plume running fore and aft, the Commandant stepped in and stood for a second smiling down. The splendor of his thickly gallooned scarlet uniform, the height and width of the epauleted shoulders, the masterful long head from the wonderful widow's peak on the brow down to the firm manly chin, all of it held her fast and breathless.

He then looked about the room, scowled a trifle at the pictures on the walls, and then with long strides went about blowing out all the candles until only two were left burning on the wine table toward the front.

"The room is magnificent," he said, breathing deeply from his effort, and offering excuses for his sudden behavior. "The place was much too brilliant, and it is you I came to see, my dear lady."

"How gallant you are, my Commandant, in everything," she replied, still breathless. "There are no such men here in Santa Fe. It is like the ways of the French Court."

"But of course, of course, my dear Casilda. For it is I who taught the French Court its ways!"

He chuckled heartily, very much pleased by this retort, and she no less enchanted by it. Banter like this, and more, melted any reserve or misgivings she might have had. He deftly opened both bottles and poured the wine into the waiting glasses. When she told him when and how it had reached Santa Fe, he began painting before her wide-open eyes the beauties of far-away France and Spain in a way that made the Frenchman's talk sound like boorish nonsense. While describing the boudoir of Marie Antoinette at Versailles, he casually looked over her shoulder toward her bedroom's doorway and suggested that she show him the rest of the house. And as though she were obeying a command, Casilda stood up and moved into the next room, he very close to her, his long arm across her shoulders.

His fingers twitched once, very lightly, and overwhelming memories of many years past surged up within her like a fever.

Her companion jerked to a stop and took in his breath sharply. They were standing just inside the bedroom. She looked up to find him eyeing the figures in the little candlelit painting above her bed. She could hear something like a growl, as an unfriendly dog growls, deep inside of him, when he muttered gruffly:

"Put out that light."

"No," she answered promptly, without thinking. "No!"

"Put out that light, I tell you!" His voice was a roar.

Casilda's heart quivered. Her limbs felt cold and weak. For the face above her was changing. As it glared down at her she saw that the handsome widow's peak looked hackly and mangy, like an angry cat's fur. What were pale blue eyes before were now a cat's sulphury yellow. One searing iris bore straight down into her, the other was turned out of balance, but she felt it also looking at her. His big smile was now a leer, drooling over the outstretched lower lip, and the large teeth were not white and even, but yellow and set apart from each other.

Satan could not look worse.

"*Jesús! María!*" she shrieked.

A flashing explosion threw her to the floor. Blinded for a second, but not knocked out of her senses, she felt some new strength in her that kept her from swooning, even though she found herself flat on the floor. From where she lay she saw eerie streaks of ill-smelling fumes streaming out into her living room and out through the open front door. A cold river of air was flowing in under that of the escaping smoke.

When at last she rose up to close the door, she could not help glancing toward the deserted Plaza. It was all white, perfectly white in the moonlight.

But leading from her threshold into what seemed infinity was a line of black marks—not of footsteps, but of cloven hooves.

Just then Captain Salazar rushed in from the side, from the direction of his quarters.

"Casilda, what happened?" he cried, grasping her shoulders. "I heard a big noise as I was coming home to bed. What happened?"

"Nothing happened, my Captain," she replied, hoping he would not see the marks on the snow. "I fainted and fell down, one of those things you men know nothing about. And I came to breathe some fresh air. That is all."

But he was already sniffing suspiciously inside the house. "Gunpowder. I smell gunpowder, Casilda, and I did hear an explosion. Dear cousin, I am going to search this house tomorrow!"

She smiled straight at him. His comical suspicion helped so much. "Dear cousin of mine, you smell what you wish to smell and hear what you wish to hear."

But this relief was not enough for her. To hide a fearful trembling that she felt returning, she asked the Captain why he had not gone to the reception.

"Oh, that," he said. "Shortly before eight a drunken soldier shot himself in the head. You know the man, *El Perico,* that vagrant from Guatemala who joined the Presidio last year. A worse foul-mouthed blasphemer I had never seen in all my life. A son of the devil he was. For almost four hours Father Hocio tried to get him to repent, but to his last breath he cursed us all and the Padre. So I could not escort you to the ball, dear cousin. Well, it is time to go, and here is Juana to assist you. God give us both a good night, and we shall see tomorrow about the gunpowder."

With this, Captain Salazar strode out the door. Casilda was vastly relieved to see that some merciful gusts of wind had meanwhile erased the trail of hooves outside. But the meaning of her sinister visitor's name and title, "Commander of the Fire," brought on such a horrible trembling once more that Juana had to assist her into bed, and also crawl in with her for the rest of the night.

Wake for Don Corsinio

THE SUDDEN NIGHT OF THE PLAINS HAD DRAPED A
black pall over the prairie-clay houses of El Piojo. But away from
the small plaza, on a faint slope to the east, a big bonfire fiercely lit
up the flat-roofed ranch house of Don Felipe. The duller light of
kerosene lamps shone dead through the front windows and open
doorways. A slight but steady nightwind carried the shrill cries of
small boys romping around the fire, and sometimes the murmur
of gruffer voices praying in unison inside the house.

Once in a while an *alabado,* yelled out dolefully from a strong
male voice, came out and boarded the nightwind. This was answered sometimes by the woeful call of a coyote out on the prairie,
and once the answer came in the faint trailing moan of a locomo-
tive from the direction of Las Vegas much further away.

It seemed as though nature as well as man, including his latest invention which had lately spun its threads of steel across San Miguel County, were all mourning the untimely passing of Don Corsinio. *Pobrecito,* everyone was saying or thinking—poor little man.

They had found him late in the afternoon after a brief but furious thunderstorm, about a mile away from El Piojo. The cold rain had soaked him to the skin, and parts of his clothes were burned off, also a sizable circle of buffalo grass around him. Nearby lay an empty smudged jug.

First the lightning must have struck him and set him afire, and then the same thunderhead belatedly took pity on him and put out the flames with a nozzle-burst of rain. This had served to chill him to death if the lightning bolt had not fully sheared away his life beforehand. Most likely he had felt no pain, for he was very drunk early that afternoon when someone saw him reeling slowly out to the prairie, jug in hand—to round up his cattle, he had said.

Poor little man. He had no cattle. He had lost all his big herds since he became a daily customer at the saloon, another institution that came with the railroad to Las Vegas and spawned little off-shoots in scattered villages like El Piojo. Since the day his lovely wife Barbara died, Don Corsinio had not only lost himself in drink but all of his earthly goods as well. Not that he had squandered it all on liquor. Somehow, his branded steers and cows had vanished from the common grazing land on the plains, and his horses, too, and his hogs and chickens from his corrals, not to mention his harnesses and tools from the sheds.

One by one the handsome furnishings which had been Barbara's pride and joy had also disappeared from the house—even a large square board with a picture of Santa Barbara painted on it.

This painting Don Corsinio himself had bartered for a week's ration from the bartender, whose wife had long coveted it.

This same woman now sat with her neighbors around the corpse, and was thinking of St. Barbara as the heavenly protector against lightning. The saintly virgin's pagan father was struck dead by a bolt from heaven after he cut off his daughter's head for being a Christian. First he had kept her locked up in a castle tower, which explained the look of her crown, like a parapet. The sword in her hand told the story of her death.

And now Don Corsinio had died like that heathen. Was he so punished for getting rid of her picture so coldheartedly, in exchange for a jug of whiskey? Anyway, Santa Barbara had come into better hands which appreciated her much more than this poor drunken fool. May he rest in peace, the woman prayed with the other mourners. Poor little man.

Don Felipe, who had offered his own house for the wake and his foodstuffs for the all-night feeding of the guests, sat quietly in one corner of the room. He also gave the dead man his own black Sunday suit and laid him out on his sheet-covered table, after shaving him with his own hands and razor. For Corsinio and Felipe had known each other since they were boys back at San Miguel del Vado, long before they got large grants on the eastern plain and moved out with their wives and other families to found El Piojo.

How different Corsinio was then, young and fine-looking, and always happy. It was he who had unwittingly named the new place, when he said that the little brown settlement on the bare prairie looked like a louse on the earth's bald head. Everyone had prospered on the new land, but none like Corsinio, who had the most uncanny luck with livestock. Some said it was because he and pretty Barbara loved each other so much.

But some lesser folks envied them and were well-primed to take advantage of Corsinio from the moment he let drink ruin him after Barbara died. Not so his boyhood friend Don Felipe, who had tried every means to save him, and his belongings also. But to no avail. Now he had done his final best for his friend, aged and dead long before his time. The shaven face and the neat black suit, and the warm candles around the corpse, made him look more like the handsome Corsinio of former days. But it was too late now. Poor little man.

Don Felipe was startled from his reverie by the *alabado* man's bursting into a screaming dirge that made the candles in the close room ward off the blow with little elbows of flame. The fellow's scrawny horseface whinnied with such soulful grief that Don Felipe could not help thinking about Corsino's cattle and horses. For the singer was at the head of the lot which had rustled all the livestock piecemeal, and peddled them at the railroad stockyard in

Las Vegas. They now sat all around the room with such doleful looks, beside their conniving sallow wives who had ransacked poor Barbara's home after her death, all joining in the chorus as if their very hearts would break.

More than once Don Felipe had complained to the sheriff and others in town, but in vain, for the singer controlled most of the votes in El Piojo as head of the secret society that did bloody penances every Holy Week. And now their chants and prayers. As if all this made up for what they had done. Don Felipe wondered what sort of warped minds these *genízaros* had.

For the families of Corsinio and Felipe, and a couple of others, were the only ones that could be called Spanish. The rest were a mixture of Plains Indian tribes, whose forebears had been captured in battle and reared in Spanish families. The singer's own parents had been a French-Canadian vagrant and his Shoshone squaw who had drifted down from Taos to San Miguel long ago. The parents and grandparents of these people had become Mexican citizens when the New World broke away from Spain, and now their children were American voters. Not all were bad by any means, but even the best were a bundle of superstitions, ancient tribal fears remembered and grafted onto Spanish Christian customs.

Unlike Felipe, Corsinio had never harbored any ill-will or disdain for these creatures, yet, see what they had done to him. *Pobrecito.*

Poor little man! Had someone ever told Don Corsinio the stir he would cause in the lives of El Piojo, he would have laughed himself to death. But now he was dead anyhow, or so his mourners thought. One of them fancied he saw an arm move slightly, and was blaming a shadow cast by the candles, when the corpse did sit up on the table of a sudden, not with a quick start, yet fast enough to charge the room with terror.

With horrified screams the men and women nearest the door scrambled madly out into the night. Those along the rear wall rushed through the adjoining kitchen, stampeding cooks and helpers before them, as well as the children playing outside. The dying bonfires sent up sprays of sparks high into the black sky when people ran through them in their eagerness to get away, and all kept running in one drove down the slope until they reached their huddled houses in the village. Bolting their doors behind them, they lit all the lamps and candles they could find and knelt down on the earthen floors to pray for the rest of the night, some women and children keeping on their wailing for hours after.

Poor Don Corsinio. For a good while he did not know where he was, sitting there on the white-sheeted table and rubbing his eyes and cheeks, then his arms and legs. But the warmth of the now jolly dipping candles felt good, although at first he did not know what caused the comfortable glow around him. As he rubbed his cleanshaven face further, and then noticed the black suit he was wearing, the white table and candles (and their meaning) began to come into focus. He called out but there was no answer. Again he called out, and this time he pronounced a name.

"Barbara!"

"Here I am, my dear Corsinio."

Through the bedroom door opposite she came toward him, repeating his name most tenderly. It was his wife, as fresh and as lovely as the first year they were married.

But why was she wearing a golden crown, shaped like a parapet of a castle tower? And why the sword in her hand? Unless it was not his wife, really, but Santa Barbara, just as she looked on that painting which he had traded for whiskey.

And yet, her face and smile were those of Barbara his wife. Even her figure was his own Barbara's, when she was big with child shortly before she died. And still, he recalled, this was also the shape of the saint on the *retablo*. The Chimayó man who had painted it long ago knew nothing of perspective and, in copying the wide flounce of the martyred virgin's regal skirt, he had made her appear what she most certainly was not in this respect.

But her voice, it was his wife's voice without a doubt. Santa Barbara or plain Barbara, he must have arrived in heaven or the borders thereof. For his good wife must have gone to heaven, surely. What disturbed him now was the fact that he himself should be there.

"You are not dead," Barbara was saying, with that smile he remembered so well. "Do you not remember this afternoon, when you went out to round up your cows, the cows that are no longer there? There was a great thundercloud overhead."

"And I was struck by lightning."

"No, no, Corsinio, it was not that. You could no longer stand up, and so you sat down on the buffalo grass. Then you decided to roll a cigarette and smoke it. This is when you fainted and the dry grass caught on fire."

"And I was burned to death?"

"No, no, Corsinio." (How well he remembered her tone of sweet forbearance when she used to say "no" twice before his name.) "My dear husband, the cloudburst put out the fire on the ground and on your clothes. But it left you so cold and stiff that the people believed you were really dead, struck dead by lightning."

"So the thundercloud saved me," Corsinio began to muse. "The great Santa Barbara, the patron of thunder and lightning— she came and saved my life. And you also, Barbara, my wife . . ."

He covered his face with both hands as if to keep a rise of sobs from shaking his head loose. For now a bitter memory came back to him, one that had lain hidden deep inside these past few years. Maybe it was the sword in her hand that brought it back.

In those happy days he had a sword like it, and which he prized the way a child does a toy. It had belonged to his grandfather as first commander of the old Spanish fort of San Miguel on the Pecos. One day he could not find it and he accused Barbara of hiding it or giving it away, for he knew that she abhorred the sight of swords and big knives. When she denied it he slapped her.

Only once he slapped her, on the cheek. It was the first and last time he ever struck Barbara, in fact, the only time he was ever angry with her. Right away he knelt down to beg her forgiveness; and she forgave him, right away.

Some days after, the baby was born, dead. And then Barbara died.

"A mere slap on the cheek never hurt anyone, except their feelings, and mine were not hurt," Barbara was saying, as she took his hands away from his face and held them in hers.

The sword was no longer in sight, but Corsinio marveled less at this than at the way she was reading his thoughts.

"You foolish boy, that slap had nothing to do with the baby's death and mine. We were to leave you anyway. Now you will never get drunk any more, Corsinio."

It was like a bright light, this revelation, which for the moment rubbed out the sputtering candles alongside and the lamps on the walls. At the same time his stomach winced and his whole frame shuddered at the very mention of getting drunk. Barbara laughed and told him that he looked hungrier than a coyote, the same words he used whenever he came home from work on the range. After removing the candles, she helped him off the table to his feet and led him into the kitchen where the *velorio* supper lay untouched. Helping him to a bench, she poured him some coffee and raised the cup to his lips. The first swallow made him feel steadier, in his head as well as his limbs. The set table before him, the entire room, began to appear more solid and real as he slowly ate the morsels of red chile and chopped meat that she kept putting in his mouth.

"You must go away from El Piojo forever, Corsinio," she was saying over his shoulder. "Go back to San Miguel, and get yourself another good woman to be your help and companion."

Corsinio turned around to reply, but she was no longer behind him or anywhere in the kitchen. Hearing footsteps in the mourning room he went in to speak to her, but ran into Don Felipe instead. Both men looked at each other in bewilderment for some moments, then embraced each other firmly and solemnly.

Don Felipe had been swept ahead by the frightened human wave when dead Don Corsinio suddenly came to life. Not that he would have stood calmly by, but he would have collected his wits about him instead of rushing pell-mell with the herd down to the village. There he found himself locked inside the bartender's house, together with this man's family and his own wife and children. These people were Spanish also, and close friends of the family, so that their coming together was no mystery.

But like their more ignorant neighbors, their hosts began lighting up every candle in the house and placing them before the painting of Santa Barbara. The lady of the house was swearing solemnly to the saint that she would be returned to Don Corsinio's house the first thing in the morning.

This gave Don Felipe some very practical ideas. Ignoring the pleas of his family and hosts, he came back to his ranch house to find his old friend walking about—in fact, the corpse partaking of the wake's refreshments. Corsinio was beginning to enjoy this, but soon grew serious and began telling all about Barbara, the dead wife and the martyr-saint, or both combined, and what they had said. Don Felipe nodded understandingly, and he also noted the sweat-beads of fever breaking out on the sick man's brow.

"This is all very good, Corsinio," he spoke at last, when the feverish man had exhausted himself talking. "But let us keep it a big secret, all that Barbara told you. Let the people keep on thinking that you really came back from the dead, and I will spread the word around that you know who robbed you. When you go back to San Miguel you will have most of your possessions back."

For some days Don Corsinio actually lay at death's door with pneumonia, carefully tended by Don Felipe and his wife, who found no difficulty in keeping visitors away. When he finally regained his health, weeks later, the unkempt poor little man had vanished. It was the young-looking Corsinio, if somewhat haggard and less bouncy, who went home one day to find all the rooms furnished as in former times.

Santa Barbara hung from the same nail, with her castlelike coronet and sword, and her queerly shaped skirt. There was a box on the table heaped with silver dollars, the price of many cattle, horses, and hogs. In the barn was a team of horses, their complete harness hanging neatly along the walls, and his own wagon.

The following day he put everything in the wagon and started out for San Miguel, Santa Barbara perched on the high seat beside him.

The Lean Years

SAN JOSÉ WAS THE PATRON SAINT OF LA CUNITA, AND the priest of Las Vegas gladly braved the prairie March winds each year to be at the fiesta. He loved the little town's setting, cradled as it was in a little hollow where the barish foothills of the great sierras came down to meet the plains. Beyond the double row of adobe houses and the chapel was a delightful small canyon with a dwarf forest of pines and scruboaks. But even this was not enough reward for a long journey on horseback in mid-March.

Perhaps it was the people themselves, some twenty families of simple folks who sat wide-eyed in the chapel listening to him tell about San José, and how his tall flowering staff was a symbol of his chaste and loving care for the Virgin Mother and her Divine Child.

It was the same sermon year after year, but, like children,

they listened to it each year as though it were for the first time. Especially young José Vera, who sat in the front bench while the other male villagers followed an unpleasant custom of crowding near the door. If not gazing intently at the preacher, José's eyes rested on the saint's statue above the altar.

An ugly monster it was, this image, if only three feet tall, the Padre could not help thinking. It shocked his French sensibilities with its stiff poise, its cheap tin coronet, its staring almond eyes on a narrow yellowish face, and, worst of all, the unreal black beard that was nothing more than a patch of black paint smeared around the thin drab lips. It shocked the sugary false baroque ideals in which he had been reared. And still, he was human enough to imagine that the people themselves did see there a beauty beyond his ken, like the mother of the ugliest brat who thinks he has the face of an angel. The image that love forms in her eyes and heart is real, and so was theirs, he reasoned. They saw, perhaps more clearly than he himself could, the true *chevalier* features of Joseph of Nazareth, a poor carpenter but also a veritable gentleman of the royal house of David.

After the Mass José Vera came to the sacristy, as he always did, and kissed the Padre's hand. His ecstasy during the sermon still glowed on his plain, kindly face.

"Padre, it was a most beautiful fiesta this year. It gets better every year. Especially your sermon about San José, it was very beautiful. And did you notice the new paper flowers on the saint's staff? And the new purple dress? They are beautiful."

Yes, he had not failed to notice that sickening mauve of the gown which common folks call purple. It rendered the lemon countenance more sulphurous. Catching himself scowling, the priest smiled benignly down at José.

"It was all most magnificent, José, and so I thanked the people for the new mud plaster all around the chapel, and for the clean white walls inside. The fine purple dress of San José, a little too short maybe, is also magnificent."

José beamed with pride, and the priest braced himself to listen with forebearance to what the youth was beginning to say. He had heard the story many times. But if José enjoyed the same sermon year after year, it was nothing but right that he himself showed some interest when the tables, or rather the pulpit, were turned around.

"My father built this chapel, years before I was born, when La Cunita was new. He also helped build all of the houses. You see, his name was also José Vera and he was a carpenter like San José, as I myself am also a carpenter and my name is José Vera. My father also made the altar, but he did not carve and paint the shells and the flowers on it. Nor did he make the image of San José. There were no *santeros* among the people who first came here to La Cunita with my father from the Rio Grande across the sierras. So they hired a man who knew how to carve and paint *santos* to come from Las Trampas. Then he went back.

"But my father and the other people, they stayed. He married my mother, and then I was born and was called José like San José and my father. My mother died when I was little and they buried her in the *campo santo,* over near the front door of the chapel. I grew up and my father taught me to be a carpenter like himself and San José. Then he died, and they buried him by my mother."

The Padre found an opening. "And now, José, it is your turn to get married, like your father. I saw Soledad looking at you from the corner of her eye during the sermon. She is a pretty girl."

The young man blushed and bowed his black head slightly. "If she will have me, I will gladly marry her."

He had no need to feel so backward, the priest thought. His regular features were pleasing and his limbs well-fashioned from hard work. He was by far the best pick in all the village for a good girl like Soledad. Surely, a word from himself to Soledad and her parents before he returned to Las Vegas would make the path smooth for the boy.

José grinned. "Thank you very much, *señor*. If Soledad will have me, I will care for her the way San José looked after blessed Mary and her little Jesus."

Then he paused and squinted at the priest, a deep problem carved on the wrinkles above his nose.

"What is it, José?"

"Padre, in your sermon this year you said something new at

the end, about another Joseph who provided for all his people. And there were seven lean years and seven years of plenty. I—I did not understand."

Neither did the other townfolk. The priest was sorry from the very moment he introduced the new idea, when he saw a thin fog of bewilderment float before their fixed gaze. Involved allegories were too much for ordinary folks, and most likely this one had fled their minds by now—except José's. José did have to remember. Now it was his duty to explain it further with all patience.

"It goes this way, my son. Joseph of Egypt, who lived long, long before Joseph of Nazareth, saved his people from starvation during seven years when no rain fell. You know what this means, when no rain falls for a long time. Therefore he was a figure of San José, who provided for Jesus and Mary in those very hard and dangerous first years, and who also provides for Christians who pray to him with confidence. Ah, what is a figure, my boy? Well, for example, if you provide for Soledad, as I know you will, then San José will have been, in a way, a figure of yourself! Do you see?"

He could plainly see that José Vera did not see too clearly. Never again would he touch on that allegory, or any other stretched comparison.

"But, Padre, what is meant by seven fat years and seven lean years?"

"Prosperous years and hard years, my son."

"Seven years of much rain and seven years of no rain?"

"Yes, yes. But they do not have to be exactly seven years each time. They could be two and five, or four and three. (*Mon Dieu,* why did I bring this on myself!)

"Only remember this, José. If you serve the Lord, and are devoted to your namesake, God will take care of you in bad years as well as in good years. Now, go with God, and have the wedding ready for June when I come here again."

The young man smiled contentedly while the Padre hid his own mingled discomfiture and relief under the Mass vestments he was pulling off over his head.

Before asking for Soledad's hand, José did over his father's little house thoroughly, something the other young swains of La

Cunita, or anywhere else in New Mexico, would have sneered at as overly particular. Besides repairing roofs and replastering walls inside and out, he remade the furniture his father had made. The tongues and grooves had loosened or broken off since his mother passed away. José re-fitted them and then carved the bedstead, the clothes chests, the sides of tables and benches, with the same stiff rosettes and shells that he saw painted on the altar of San José. Not to be caught short, he built a small cradle, carved with cherub heads that could be easily mistaken for apples, and he also made a little low table with half a dozen toy chairs to go with it.

Soledad's father and mother put on surprise when José made his formal plea one bright spring morning. Since he had no parents to do it for him, nor any relatives like the other intermarried folk of La Cunita, he brought along as spokesman an old unkempt fellow by the name of Urbán, the village midwife's husband. The choice had nothing to do, in José's mind, with the cradle and the toy furniture. It so happened that Urbán was the only man on hand at the moment the shy groom had worked up enough courage. The rest of the townsmen were out working their fields or looking over their livestock on the prairie.

"*Señor y Señora,*" Urbán began orating through his bleached and stained shaggy whiskers. "Unworthy though I am, the honor and pleasure have fallen upon me to bring you tidings of grievous import and tremendous consequences for the future, which God alone in his temerarious ways can foresee, since there comes a time in the life of male members of the human genus—one worthy sample for whom I speak in the unfortunate circumstances of his being bereft of progenitors to plead for him . . ."

The florid prelude was cut short by the parents' quick acceptance of José, and joyful Soledad was summoned from the kitchen, where she had been spying and listening, to have her moist hand placed in José's with archaic blessings uttered in centuries–old Castilian rhymes that were almost unintelligible from being worn round and smooth at the edges.

The Padre's summer visit came early in June, and La Cunita was ready for him with many baptisms to be performed after the Mass, and some spots to be blessed in the graveyard. He also found the entire apse of the chapel silvery gold with *capulín* blossoms (like lilacs of France, but pale yellow and more delicately fragrant), the native chokecherry that filled a moist ravine next to the pine forest further up the narrow valley. And he was proud to see how charming José and Soledad looked, kneeling before him on the altar step.

The whole village was there rejoicing, as were the dogs which cannot bear a dwelling emptied of all human life, just as they attended, as one, the four yearly Masses, the fiesta of San José, or the wakes and priestless burials whenever one of the villagers departed from La Cunita for the first (and last) time in his short or long life.

After the nuptial Mass the bridal couple was led to the bride's home by two musicians, one man sawing away jerkily on a rawhide violin, and his companion strumming a cracked paunchy guitar that seemed to have been sired by a bullfiddle. The cooks had left the chapel early, and the bride's parents had been rushed home before the procession started to receive the wedded pair at their door. There José and Soledad knelt on the threshold to kiss the old couple's leathery hands, which blessed them in turn with the sign of the cross. Then they went in, followed by the elder guests, to partake of a little drink and sweet cinnamon biscuits before being called to the wedding board.

There was no wine, and the Lord was not there, visibly, to fill their waterpots as had happened with similar gentle folks long ago. Here the season was much too brief for grapes, a fruit which only the older folks remembered years back in the valley of the Rio Grande. The small drink offered was sugared water, lime-soured with the crushed green beads of the *lemita* bush, which grew among the scruboaks. There also was another drink, foul-tasting and fiery, which only Urbán, who made it, was able to relish. The tougher males managed to down a small mouthful of it, to be polite to their host and appear strong and brave to their women-folk.

After sundown everyone followed the musicians to what was called the *sala de fandango.* This was a lengthy old adobe room used now and then for dances. It was roofed over with log beams and a foot of earth, just like the chapel and the dwellings, except that it was in much more need of repair. Against the rear wall a canopied throne had been fixed up with bedsheets and shawls, where the bride and groom were to preside all evening, after they had led the first dance. It was here that it happened.

Earlier in the evening thin streams of fine dry dust had begun sifting down on the necks of dancing couples and of elderly people on benches along the walls. It came from the pounding of running feet above. Boys who were not old or brave enough to take a dancing partner, had propped a ladder outside to chase one another up and down the flat earthen roof. Tired of shooing them away time and again, the older men had resigned themselves to an annoyance which they themselves recalled causing many years before. The fiddle and guitar were still screeching and thumping hours later, the older folks were still prancing and twirling on the hard earth floor, the boys were still running up and down the ladder and stamping all over the dirt roof, when the rotten old beam over the canopy broke in two and let down an avalanche of dusty soil upon José and Soledad.

José was pulled out unhurt, but the longer end of the snapped *viga* had slipped down heavily onto Soledad's lap. Grimy as he was from head to foot, the groom himself carried her to her mother's house like a broken doll, except that she breathed and moaned faintly with pain, and her voice seemed to come from far away.

The fiesta of San José came around once again, and found Soledad motionless in bed at her father's house. Many weeks later, in June, José brought the first chokecherry blossoms to Soledad's bedside. For almost the entire summer, last year, she had lain motionless, without knowing that her husband sat every night through at her side, or that during the day her mother and the town midwife swathed her hips and thighs with new poultices and bandages. Then she returned, slowly and hesitantly at first, to become aware of José's hands around her own, and by Christmas the midwife proudly predicted that she would be up and dancing with José when the March fiesta of San José arrived once more.

But though Soledad's color came back, and the life in her eyes from a faraway land behind them, her little body from the waist down stayed pinned down by the weight of an invisible *viga*. Because she could now eat and sleep well, the midwife sagely foretold that she would walk home on the day of her wedding anniversary and sleep in the bed that José had carved with shells and flowers.

However, on the day that José came in with the first choke-cherry blossoms, Soledad lay bedridden still, sobbing deeply among her pillows. Her mother and father stood gravely by. Urbán was there, too, at the side of his herbwoman, who was also crying to herself, for she had finally admitted the truth to herself and shamefacedly told it to the girl and her parents, little realizing that her restoring of half of Soledad to health had been miracle enough.

Now the midwife said bluntly to José: "She will never walk again. Her hips have shrunk—like this—like a little boy's. She is your wife, and not your wife."

José halted and stared at the woman. Her quiet voice burst clear into his ears like a shout. It seemed as though he had been living in a dream for twelve months now, and that he really had heard no one speak out loud until this moment.

Soledad's father began shaking him gently. "My son, José, it must be the will of God. Our daughter can stay with us always, her mother and myself, and Urbán's wife to help. But we leave that to your own judgment, son. She is your wife."

"Your wife, and not your wife . . ." José felt Soledad's eyes upon him. They were wet, but still they firmly locked into his own stare and held it. It was the same full look she had given him when the Padre called them man and wife, yet somehow not the same, not quite the same. Or else it was he who was different.

"Let her decide," he stammered at last.

Soledad shook her head. "You are the man, José. You decide."

José gestured, but the words lodged in his throat.

"No, not right away. Come back tomorrow morning," Soledad said, closing her eyes and letting her head sink back into the pillows.

José hung his head for a moment, and then trudged out the door.

No one was in sight the length of the whole street. Most of the people were out on the fields, plowing, sowing, mending fences and corrals. They were always doing that. He remembered the day Urbán spoke for her hand. Today there was no one to speak to, no father and mother to turn to, the way Soledad could. He found himself by the chapel, not by happenstance as in romances, but by instinct, and went in to kneel before San José. He knelt there for a long time, but said nothing, thought nothing. His mind was numb, his lips were dumb.

And San José himself was no different. The wooden statue stared and stared into space with his even almond eyes outlined with black and white on his narrow yellowish face. His black beard, more like tar dabbed around from ear to ear, made him look more impersonal, as if he did not care about either joy or sorrow. He had stared this way over the crude coffins of José's father and mother, and a year ago over his own head and the white-veiled brow of Soledad. If he would only bow a bit, or shift the tiny Infant from his left arm, or move one of his stiff cornstalk legs and big splayed feet that showed beneath his purple gown. Now he remembered the Padre saying it was a little too short. If he would only shake the tall staff in his right hand and rustle the paper flowers that the women tied to the top of it every feast day.

José did hear a paper rustling in the bare stillness of the chapel, but it was only an angry wasp trapped at one of the windows.

He went home, at last, to find Urbán waiting at his hand-carved table. A jug stood at his elbow. His browntoothed grin among the mottled red and gray whiskers looked much more human that St. Joseph's. There was a live friendly gleam in his red-rimmed hazel eyes. The older man motioned to the bench, and José sat down beside him.

"Here, this is what you need," Urbán said, leaning closer to offer him a drink. "This is what any man needs. I learned the trick from an *Americano* in Taos, years before you were born, before we came to live here. He was from a place called Kentuck, bless his soul, and he was killed in a brawl. Great man. Do you know that the Indians have had corn for thousands of years, and all they made was cornmeal? Then our own people have grown corn for hundreds of years, and all they could make was cornbread and *posole*. But this grand *señor* from the States knew how to find the very spirit of the corn, the only medicine for a he-man's sickness. Here, take some . . ."

José had pulled back and turned away holding his breath. People had good cause to say that Urbán stank like a dead cow out on the prairie. Outside, the prairie breeze helped to make him tolerable, but folks stole away from his side at fandangos and in the chapel. Thinking it was the jug from which the young man shrank, he urged him on, and José, ashamed of his unkind gesture, took the jug and raised it to his mouth. As if the taste were not torment enough, the large swallow that he hastily downed cut a burning gash all the way down his throat. Coughing and gasping he got up and threw himself face down upon the bed.

Sometime later, José began to notice that the tightness in his head was gone. He felt a knot in his breast becoming untied. Sitting up, he saw that Urbán was gone. But the jug was still there. Yes, there, he thought, was another good friend. Harsh and ill-smelling though it was, like its maker, it had the same understanding heart. And if one swallow could heal the head so quickly, others would reach the heart. Several pulls at the jug later, José felt the room swaying. Then his stomach jumped up as if trying to escape through his mouth. He rushed out retching through the door, and then came back and flung himself upon the bed.

He had lain quiet for some time when the sound of footsteps made him sit up. Thinking it was Urbán who had returned, he called him but got no answer. He could barely see for the throbbing on his pate and temples, as though someone were using his own hammers on them. After he got used to the afternoon glow in his eyes, he kept on frowning and shaking his head at what he saw.

For it was the image of San José standing in the middle of the floor.

What sacreligious thought had prompted Urbán to play such a prank on him? One did not play with the saints.

"I have come to help my namesake in his troubles," said the little statue.

Its lips actually moved. José caught a glimpse of moist white teeth as it spoke.

"Oh, my head, my head," José moaned to himself. "I will never touch that poison again."

"You say well, my boy. Never do it again."

This time José leaned over closer. It, *he,* had spoken again.

And he was smiling, a real fatherly smile, so much like his own departed father's. The straight swaths of black paint that were his beard still looked like black paint, or tar, but the countenance was more human. He was all alive, even though he was no more than three feet high.

"My boy, I heard your silent prayer in the chapel. You have always been a good lad, and I have come to help you. Take Soledad for your wife, José, bring her home with you. Don't you love her any more?"

"But, *Señor San José,* you do know what all this has done to me. Oh, yes, I still love her . . ."

"Then take her, son. And remember that I know, I know perfectly."

The saint began to recall the Padre's yearly talks on his feast, how Joseph himself had been sorely troubled but finally had taken Mary to wife, all for the sake of the Child, and he pointed to the Infant Jesus on his arm.

There shone a light about him when he said this, and the white paper flowers on his staff began to look and smell like real flowers, though what kind, José could not tell.

"Oh, if only I had a child like Him," said José, entranced.

"Let Soledad be your child, as well as your spouse, my dear boy. And also remember that there are lean years for those who serve the Lord, sometimes very lean and hard years; but He also will provide the fat and prosperous ones. Good-by, son."

With this the saint swiveled stiffly toward the door and waddled away like a duck on his ungainly wide feet. Click-clack, click-clack, they went . . .

José fell back on the bed and did not wake up until next morning.

Soledad was waiting, all cleaned up and propped up among her pillows when José walked in. She knew what he was going to say, and do, from the manner in which he strode across the high threshold, his eyes eagerly seeking hers. His face was pale and drawn, as from sickness, but his eyes were sharp and hearty.

"I am taking you home now," he almost shouted, bending down to kiss her warmly. "You are my wife—and my baby!"

Her mother began to wail with joy, and hugged her son-in-law tight around the waist, while her father embraced his shoulders. The midwife knelt down and kissed his hands. Then, after promises of everlasting help from the parents and the herb-woman, José lifted his wife up, bed-covers and all, and started out for home. The others formed a little bridal procession, marching in time to the music in their hearts. Urbán, the only man on the street, as usual, took off his tattered hat and rubbed his eyes with cracked knuckles. By evening the whole village had gone to the Vera house to wish them good health and every good thing.

For more than three years José and Soledad Vera were an unending joy to themselves and to La Cunita. He fashioned big comfortable chairs for her, one before the window in the front room, another in the kitchen, and the third in his workshop, so that she could watch and chat with him as he worked with his tools. From the front window she had a full view of the village, a wooded spur of foothills, and the vast sea of prairie beyond where the billowing clouds formed pictures endlessly.

Folks never tired of seeing José bundling her up carefully on his wagon whenever he had to go out to tend his field or cut timber in the small forest. When they made calls on the neighbors, or joined the villagers in the chapel for rosary or hymns, Soledad made her appearance in his strong arms, and the very sight brought out tenderness from the most hardened.

But Soledad began to grow paler and thinner, too gradually at first for others to see. José had begun to notice, however, a dimming of the sparkle in her eyes, and in her laughter. She wept in her sleep. Moreover, some unthinking housewives had begun telling her how lucky she was in being free of the pains and burdens of having and rearing children, in not having to strain her arms and back day after day in household work. They really were seeking comfort from her, but she took all this for slurs on her not being able to do these very things for her own husband. Then one day José came in with a bruised eyebrow and swollen jaw. He said a horse had thrown him. But the same women had to tell her the truth not long after.

A pair of young villagers, who had grown to like Urbán's corn whiskey, had openly poked fun at José for being only a quarter-husband, and he had been obliged to trounce them.

José and Soledad had their first quarrel when she upbraided him for not telling her the true story.

Something else started bothering José. It began the day he was fixing a cupboard in the kitchen of the young and chubby widow Casillas. Not that anything wrong was said or done. She had merely offered to hold down a shaky board he was sawing, and the board was not too long either. That was all.

It showed that he had been unaware of other women, healthy women, besides Soledad. Now when she slipped into a pouting mood he did nothing to cheer her up, as he had done before. Even the sight of the cradle and toy furniture he had made five years before began to anger him inside, especially since the night he got up to fetch Soledad some water, and skinned his shin on the cradle's edge.

Although he had long known (Urbán had mentioned it) that the general merchant's wife in Las Vegas would pay good money for such objects, José had not thought of selling the cradle and the other pieces until now. In fact, he had never been interested in going to Las Vegas, to see with his own eyes the strange and unbelievable things that Urbán and others of the men talked about. The railroad had reached the town some months ago, a string of great wagons pulled at great speed by a round iron box built like a bison and filled with fire. This he did yearn to see.

Now was the time to get rid of the toys and some other large pieces he had made, for money which was becoming more and more necessary of late in trading for food or fabrics.

José tersely told Soledad what he was doing when he loaded the wagon one evening. Early the next morning he left her at her mother's house and kept on following the twin ruts over the prairie that led but to one place at the end of two days. Once there, he was not disappointed by the noisy monster that hissed from hunched shoulders to rump with mighty snorts of steam; save for the big funnel of a smokestack, it fitted perfectly with Urbán's picture of a buffalo. Then there were other things, too many to dwell upon at once, but none to compare so far with the train at the depot.

Of course, there was the big store, a house of treasure, and no less wonderful were the kindliness of the baldheaded merchant, with a nose that seemed purposely built for his heavy-rimmed spectacles, and his little fat wife with a very pretty white face and glossy black hair, like a blackbird's coat. She gave him a stack of silver dollars for the cradle and small chairs, and ordered some more made. Her husband was more critical of the larger adult furniture, but gave him many more silver dollars, and offered to buy more when he brought them.

While waiting for a passenger train which, the station agent told him, would arrive late in the afternoon, José stopped at another store, one with very interesting smells. He could not read the sign above the door, but he knew what it was as soon as he went in, again from Urbán's descriptions. There was only the man behind the bar. Behind him was a great big mirror, as big as a lake, which made rows of bottles in front of it appear twice as many as there actually were. This man had a kind face, too. He asked José if he wanted a shot of whiskey. Remembering Urbán and his jug, he winced and shook his head. Then some wine?

José had heard how good wine tasted, but the only wine he had ever seen, and from a distance, was the purplish red liquid which the Padre poured into the chalice in the chapel of San José. He pointed to a bottle of the same color, and the bartender poured him a small glassful of burgundy. He liked it. It was like the aftertaste of ripe chokecherries, but *capulín* never rose like a luscious vapor and lingered in one's head. It was a far cry from Urbán's raspy slop. The man said there were sweeter-tasting wines, and José tried the muscatel, then the tokay. Yes, he liked them all very much better.

Two women came in and talked briefly with the bartender in a strange language. Before leaving, each one downed a small glassful of amber liquor. What amazed José was not only the assured poise of their husky frames sheathed in black silk, but the fairness of their faces and necks, the golden sheen of their thick hair, like clean pine shavings. As the man poured José a small glassful of angelica, he told him about these ladies whom the iron bison had brought.

Their place stood behind the general store, the first house with a porch, on the street to the left.

José staggered out, not too dizzy in his head, but unable to control his legs for a while. After he succeeded in taming them, a masterful feeling welled up in his chest, as when one brought a wayward team of horses into line. Yes, palomino horses, with manes like clean pine shavings. He walked slowly up toward the store and around it. But instead of taking the left-hand street he wandered to the right. The first house had a porch, and also a white picket fence in front—and something else that brought him to a halt with a most pleasant shock.

It was a little garden of flowers, most of them stalks almost as tall as himself, each hung with rows of paper-like cups. On some stalks they were red, on others pink, but most were white. Only they were not paper. José reached out to touch one and a bee buzzed out. The house door opened at the same time and a little aged woman came forth, but not angry like the bee.

"You like my flowers, son," she said.

José grinned and nodded. "I never saw such beautiful flowers before, except in a dream, once."

That vision of five years ago came back to him with a sweetness more overpowering than that of the wine. Indeed, it melted away any wine-headiness that remained.

"You know, *señora*," said he, amazed by the memory. "You know, they look just like the staff of Saint Joseph back home, in the chapel of La Cunita."

"That is what our people call them, *varas de San José*," the lady explained. "The *Americanos* who brought them call them hollyhocks."

He did not like the English name. It sounded like Urbán clearing his throat out loud in church. But that did not spoil their beauty for him, or their meaning to himself, so well described by their Spanish name. He next wanted to know if the seeds cost much money. He had plenty of silver dollars now.

The lady laughed. Telling him to wait, she went into the house and promptly returned with a paper sack full of dried pods and seeds, enough to sow a small cornfield. They needed little care, she said, and the second year brought hundreds of flowers, and seeds to throw away.

Clutching the sack to his breast, José thanked the kind woman profusely and went back to the store, where he began picking out dresses and shawls for Soledad and her mother, and new wide-brimmed beavers for Urbán and his father-in-law. And things for the midwife, too. The merchant and his wife tried to steer him away to cheaper and more useful items, but stopped when José began telling them all about Soledad. The merchant's eyes moistened behind the thick quoits of glass perched on his nose, and the lady cooed sweetly while big tears ran down her cheeks. They both fixed up a box of canned and packaged foodstuffs for him besides, and José drove back to La Cunita thinking that his silver dollars had paid for everything he brought along.

Soledad had sunk into a deep dark mood after José left. His taking away the cradle and the children's table and chairs had hurt the most. She was sure that he had done it to spite her. But she began to miss him the very first day, since she had never been without him these five years. By the fourth day she had absolved him of all blame, knowing that it was herself who had widened the rift between them of late. How to make things right without angering him all over again became her chief worry.

Next day every misgiving vanished, when she saw his wagon draw up to her father's doorway. The look in his face, and the way he leaped down to the ground and then strode over the threshold, recalled that morning when he first picked her up with the bed-covers and carried her home from this very room.

Everyone gasped with awe at the gifts he brought. But Soledad became much more interested in the paper sack full of seeds, for she saw that José prized them more than anything he had ever owned. Her delight when he finished a neat picket fence in front of their home brought his old merry self to full bloom. The following summer the little yard brimmed with big leaves like a dark cabbage patch, but José already saw the bright swaying stalks and knew that Soledad saw them with him. That winter, though, she began to grow visibly paler and thinner, and both knew what it meant.

If only she could live long enough to see the first Saint Joseph's staffs.

She did. It was a dwarf forest of snow-white bells that filled her soul with their own beauty that last June, and with the beauty of the look in her husband's eyes. She used to sit unwearyingly at the window, watching them nod gently in the breeze from the prairie, and they were looking in through the window when José found her dead one quiet day.

He buried her next to his father and mother. There were very few of the people at the funeral, for most of the village folk had left La Cunita, including Urbán and his wife. This past year some tall blond men with jowls like coxcombs had come with long-worded papers from Santa Fe, saying that all the prairie around La Cunita now belonged to them. The inhabitants of La Cunita could no longer graze their cattle and sheep on the land. The sheriff of Las Vegas who came with them sheepishly said that they were right, and nothing could be done about it. After getting a pittance for the plots on which their houses stood, the men began taking their families to Las Vegas. They found steady work right away and began replacing the Chinese coolies in the railroad section gangs.

Then José and the very last remnants also left. Because he was very clever with tools, José was hired to work in the roundhouse, where he became intimate with the once awesome iron buffalos which, like human beings, ran down and needed expert care. He also found a new wife in Las Vegas, a very good woman, most devoted and healthy, who knew how to make the best of his growing wages, which were needed for a family that kept pace with them.

This fine woman also shared his love for flowers, and grew hollyhocks with the reddest blossoms, and also pink ones and white ones. But even the white ones had red and purple centers.

A Desert Idyll

SUNSET, GOLD AND CRIMSON, PAINTED THE DESERT; A low bleating now and then arose from the mesa—all else was silence. Shadows began to lengthen behind the sage and cedar that studded the golden desert, and the blushing banks and cliffs, trembling in crimson and orange, faced the lavish brush of the fiery painter.

The infrequent bleating became more distinct. Sharply in contrast, a loud bark issued from the mesa, at the crest of which appeared a flock of sheep. Behind it and around the erect form of an Indian boy frolicked a shaggy dog. The boy was short and thin, no older than ten, with his thick raven hair bobbed at the temple, the rest being tied at the back with threads of red wool. His shirt, after the manner of the Navajo, was of black velvet, girt with a belt of large, silver shells and reaching to above his knees over a pair of white trousers. Steadily he gazed at the setting sun and his heart beat with emotion as he chanted the hymn of the Sun God, the same song that his forefathers sang centuries before. For what greater spectacle was there to the children of the American desert than the glory of a western sunset? Surely, they thought, the sun, so bright and so good, must be God! These were the thoughts in the mind of little Nop-ha. The sun was God! His father had said so. But, then, other thoughts arose in conflict. Had not his mother secretly told him that the sun was not God, and that there was One who ruled all, even the sun? Thus pondering, Nop–ha, the Navajo shepherd boy, followed the sheep down the slope of the mesa into the lowland.

At the entrance of the solitary hogan, the typical Navajo hut, stood Nop-ha with a troubled heart. In a corner lay his sick mother, and, as the sinking rays of the sun lit the boy's features, she read on them a feeling of sadness.

"Nop-ha, my boy," she whispered very softly, "what makes my man so sad? His big father will return in a few days!"

"Oh, nothing, little mother," he replied.

Painfully sitting up among her blankets, she stretched her arms toward him.

"Come, my warrior! Come, tell little mother what makes him sad."

And the lad drew close, and told her all, but then a look of gloom fell upon the poor mother.

"Yes, my son," she sighed deeply, "there is only one God. When little mother was a girl, she learnt this at the mission school. The Padres told her of Jesus, Maria, and of the saints and angels."

Long she talked to him about God. She narrated to him the life of the Redeemer and dwelt particularly upon the Blessed Sacrament. Sadly she unfolded her life to Nop-ha, how she had been wedded to a man who hated the Padres and lived far from them. Then she produced a little picture of a beautiful man holding a little babe.

"That is San Antonio, Nop-ha mine. The Child is He Who was born on earth, killed by savage men, and then rose alive into the blue sky. But, as I told you, He is still with us. His Padres have Him for Whom I have longed all this year."

"Mother," broke in the boy, "give Nop-ha this picture. To-morrow at sunset he shall pray to this Antonio to bring the Child to little mother." She smiled weakly and pressed the thing to her lips, then to his.

Again on the following evening, the sun repeated the spectacle of the preceding day. Only to Nop-ha, standing on the same mesa, the gold seemed more golden and the crimson on the cliffs shone redder. Toward the ball of fire he stretched out the arms and prayed:

"Oh, Thou Who made the glorious sun, send San Antonio to little mother! Tell him to bring Thee to her!" Full of love and zeal, his little throat poured out the rhythmic chant of the Sun-God. It was to the true God he sang the only song he knew, the song his father had taught him.

As the last note died away, a shout echoed from the road below. There stood one of those wagons brought by the Americanos, an automobile. In response to another call, Nop-ha ran down the slope. Of a sudden, he stopped in surprise, for out of the car stepped a figure in brown robes, with a white cord around his waist.

"A beautiful song, my boy!" said the mysterious one, "but where does this road go?"

"San Antonio," the lad exclaimed, "have you brought Him?"

"Brought whom? I am not San Antonio, little boy, I am Padre Jerome from the Mission."

The boy's countenance fell. Then, on second thought, he drew out the picture. On seeing it, the Franciscan burst out in a merry peal of laughter. Kindly pinching the lad's cheek, he asked:

"What do you want with St. Anthony, my little Navajo?"

"Mother is sick," Nop-ha answered, "and she wants San Antonio to bring Him to her." And he pointed to the picture of the Child Jesus.

"I have him with me," rejoined the priest, "lead me to her."

As the sun began to finish its masterpiece upon the desert, a flock of bleating sheep moved down the slope of the mesa, but this time a shaggy dog frolicked around a joyous Indian boy and a happy Franciscan friar.

The Tesuque Pony Express

UP THE CEDARED HILLS AND ALONG THE WINDING highway, a little black mustang paced its way at its own sweet ease. Swaying in rhythm to the horse's motion, a lad of ten sat lazily upon its back. Faded blue jeans, a patched, white shirt, and a tattered hat made up the armor of this knight of the sage-country, all of which Juanito wore with a grace; for was he not enjoying his trip? Juanito always did enjoy this short tour from the Tesuque Valley up to old Santa Fe.

There were reasons for this enjoyment. Besides his liking to be in the "city," there was a self-consciousness in him akin to pride. Juanito was the trusty family messenger or, to put it nearer to his own view of it, he was a sort of "Pony Express." There were many necessary articles which had to come from Santa Fe, and he was ever ready for his venture abroad. This happened to be one of the weekly pilgrimages of Juanito.

By this time, the pony and boy were well on their way. Juanito, turning around on his Rosinante, vainly tried to catch a glimpse of the home valley. Only cedars and piñons and a distant expanse of grotesque sand–cliffs met his gaze. Before him, a panorama of beauty was steadily unfolding itself—soon the city would be in sight. Usually Juanito drank in all this beauty. Now, however, he was occupied in trying to recall a certain errand which had been entrusted to him. Though he recalled distinctly all other errands he had to perform, this one charge seemed to be near his memory—yet he could not grasp it.

Of a sudden, upon an elevated promontory, around which the road began to wind down into the Santa Fe valley, appeared the immense "Cross of the Franciscan Martyrs." Just as suddenly, Juanito remembered what he had all the while tried to recall. "I mustn't forget Grandma Rita's candle to St. Anthony," he told himself, and began to search for the dime she had given him for the purpose. This was an errand he dared not forget. Old Rita had to have vigil light burning before St. Anthony at the Cathedral, and her dime was always waiting for the Tesuque Pony Express to go to town. Juanito, indeed, had almost forgotten this special charge many a time, but had not failed so far. This time, it was the Martyrs' Cross that reminded him of St. Anthony.

All this while he had been searching for that dime—but to no avail. He had lost it! How could he now buy a candle for San Antonio? What would Rita say? He began to plan—no, he would not tell the old lady a lie. She would read the truth out of his eye; she was good at such things. One only remedy remained, and that was to ask the saint himself for help.

But Juanito had grown a little skeptical, despite his age and size, as far as burning vigil lights was concerned. Grandma Rita seemed to get no help for all her devotions. For instance, the hail had destroyed the bean crop; the frost had killed the young apricots; the chile peppers were not as numerous as those of the preceding year; even Rita's rheumatism was getting worse every day. Oh, well! he thought; the old woman knew better. And he prayed.

Just around the bend of the highway, in full view of the large concrete cross above him and the city below, the little mustang halted. Juanito's meditations were interrupted by a call at his side, "Say, kid, are you in much of a hurry?"

Amid a clump of sage on the road embankment stood a lady in a multihued smock. She had been folding together what seemed to be a camp stool, a parasol, and an easel. A box of shining lead tubes still lay open at her feet. "I see you're going into town." The lady smiled and winked. "Could you do me a favor, if you're not in a hurry?"

"Sure," the boy assented. "I got plenty time. I just go to this and to that store and I am finished. Papa wants something, mama wants something, and sister wants a pair of silk stockings, a—"

"Well, I declare," said the lady, in mild surprise. "And is that all?"

"Well," Juanito added, "I also gotta light St. Anthony a candle in the church for my grandma."

The artist laughed. "I think you're all right, young man. Will you take this stuff to the Acequia Madre for me?" and she gave a house number.

"Oh, sure, sure," he said eagerly. The lady laid her things before him on the saddle. "Tell the people there," she said, "that I won't be back until this evening. And here is a dollar for you, kid, for being a good little boy!" With this, she also slapped the horse and, as it trotted down the hill, waved at the happy boy.

After the "Pony Express" had gone its several rounds throughout the town, Juanito drove his steed before the Cathedral, dismounted, and went in. A few minutes later he emerged, climbed upon his faithful pony, and rode away, back to old Tesuque. Before St. Anthony's altar two more vigil lights were burning.

My Ancestor—Don Pedro

NERVOUSLY ROLLING HIS TENTH CIGARETTE, DON JUAN de Herrera sat on his easy chair beneath an ancient apricot tree. On a bench sat the honorable Dr. J. Payton Smiggs, an Eastern literary magazine editor and a noted student in national archeology and history. His spectacles were perched saucily on his eagle nose, and the lips under his carefully trimmed mustache were held in a pose of obvious impatience and contempt.

"Don Juan," spoke the editor, "I have heard much about you and have spared a little of my precious time to come and hear a story from your own lips."

The old don raised his eyebrows and shrugged his shoulders. Of course, the visitor had heard of him. He knew that. And he was aware of the stir he was creating among men of letters with his interesting and historically authentic tales of ancient New Mexico.

As he knew English very well, having been, as people talked, a great politician and legislative interpreter in territorial days, many were the authors and historians that came to him in quest of facts and material. Don Juan knew all this; and he also knew that a certain man was attacking the truth and authenticity of his anecdotes, and that man was Dr. J. Payton Smiggs.

"Furthermore, I am sure you have heard of me more than once," Smiggs continued, very prim and sophisticated.

"Yes, yes," at last spoke the don, "it is true. I have heard of you." There was a sly twinkle in his eye as he said this. "But what do you desire me to speak about? The Indians—no? Or maybe of the Padre Padilla—"

"What I would like from your own lips, Don Juan, is an old, old story, true of course, that you have not told thus far. Some little incident that lies hidden in some secluded nook of your memory."

"Yes, yes, Professor Smiggs," the old man assented, the same twinkle in his eye, "I have one good story for you. It is about my ancestor, Don Pedro de Herrera. You have heard of him, maybe—yes?"

"I do not recall the name," said Dr. Smiggs, very composed and aloof.

"Well, that does not matter. But you remember from your books that year when Captain Juan de Zaldivar arrived at Acoma, the City of the Sky—1598, no? Yes, in that year and in that expedition came my ancestor, Don Pedro de Herrera. He was my grandfather's great great grandfather."

Dr. Smiggs cocked an ear with a little more interest. The historical beginning of the narrative was correct so far.

"Captain Zaldivar, as your historians know, left San Gabriel with thirty men to join and re-enforce the troops of the great Oñate. On reaching the foot of the City of the Sky, he was invited by the Indians to visit their town up on the high rock. Mind you, Oñate had narrowly escaped death here by treachery just two months before. But Zaldivar knew nothing about it, even if he was acquainted with Indian treachery. Anyway, he let himself be deceived for the first time in his life, and he went up with sixteen men.

"My ancestor, Don Pedro, was one of the sixteen. Ah, he was a brave and noble young man of twenty summers. He had but come from old Castile and had not yet met my grandfather's great great grandmother in San Gabriel. As you see, he was inexperienced with women, much less with Indians. Ah! you smile—it is very true, yes? As I was saying, he had not the experience, but he could fight. All Spanish can fight, true. But he was what the Americans call the 'star' with the rapier. What is more queer, he was left-handed. But, perhaps, the story is not interesting enough for the gentleman, no?"

The editor was on the point of falling headlong from the bench, so much was he bending forward and stretching his neck to catch every word. "Continue, please," he said.

"The town up near the sky was so strange, so full of wonders, the people so hospitable, that the Spaniards forgot whatever suspicions they might have had; and by degrees they scattered all over the place. Ah, Mister, there was the grand mistake! The vile sons of the devil had been waiting only for this. And when they were scattered so, the Indian chief gave the war yell, and the men and the women and the children took stones and flints and clubs and they fell with savage madness upon the poor, unsuspecting Christians. Ah, Professor, that was a sad day, as you know from history. The brave soldiers fought back, indeed; but the Indians were too close and too many. There was no time for the reloading of the muskets. Yet, there was no coward blood, friend, among these sons of Spain!

"But I must tell you about my ancestor, Don Pedro. While each soldier was hacking away at the foe with his musket, hitting here and missing there, Don Pedro stood by his Captain, Don Juan de Zaldivar. He fought for him, they fought for each other, and at last the Captain fell. My ancestor was left alone, but his rapier was more than enough for the pagans. He saw nine of his dear comrades fall, one by one, but brave to the last. He also saw the five other survivors, five besides himself, slowly retreat to the edge of the cliff, fighting all the way. And, as he himself stood at bay, surrounded by the savage mob, he saw the five leap backward into the abyss behind the horrid precipice. He heard the victorious cries of their pursuers and then turned all his attention to those around him. Don Pedro was the only Spaniard alive on the cliff city of Acoma, and he resolved to remain alive as long as he could!"

Meanwhile, the old don watched Mr. Smiggs. The professor was literally sweating. His spectacles had slid off his nose into his lap.

"Now, my ancestor, Don Pedro, had to fight a whole population single-handed. But he acted admirably. Shouting an invocation to the Virgin, he fell upon the Indians with all his might and he forced his way to the top of a house. Bleeding from a hundred wounds, he set his back to a corner and there faced the savage charge of the enemy. Ah, friend, never in history did a single sword do such noble work. Why, that rapier in his left hand was red—red! It stuck here, it pushed here—poof! like the head of a rattlesnake made of lightning. Brave warriors fell, fanatic pagan priests tumbled at Don Pedro's feet; even chiefs and governors, their heads waving with a thousand eagle-feathers, found the point of that darting, deadly, magic, red rapier in their breasts and in their throats. Their whoops and heathen incantations were stopped short by the noble sword of the besieged Christian knight.

"But do not think that my ancestor did not receive a wound for every wound he gave; for stones and sharp rocks crashed against his shining breastplate. Rocks that hit the stone and adobe wall behind him rebounded and fell with terrific force on his helmet. Arrows pierced his poorly protected arms and legs. Weaker and weaker became Don Pedro; his head began to swim. But still his unconquered left arm wielded that rapier with a deadly force.

"'Spare his life,' shouted a medicine-man to the Indians in their language. 'He is brave—he is enchanted, bewitched. Save him for the snake-god!' But Don Pedro stood no longer on his feet. He had sunk to his knees, and a young warrior, the nearest to him, leaped forward and drove his spear deep into the gallant soldier's throat. Thus died my ancestor, Don Pedro de Herrera."

The editor was no longer sitting on the bench. He stood in nervous excitement, his pencil jotting down hurried shorthand characters in his note-book. Now that the old man had stopped speaking, he looked up in astonishment.

"You say, Don Juan, that Don Pedro was your ancestor?"

"Yes, yes, Mr. Smiggs, and a very noble young man."

"But how could he be your ancestor when he had not yet met your grandfather's great great grandmother, who was then in San Gabriel?" queried the editor.

"Ah, Professor, that is the sad thing. My ancestor had to die so young and so inexperienced before he could tell us that!"

Dr. J. Payton Smiggs caught the meaning of the sly sparkle in the old don's eye. Closing his note-book and picking up his spectacles from the ground, he absent-mindedly plucked an apricot from an overhanging branch, and walked away.

The Colonel and the Santo

THE COLONEL HAD SAID LITTLE SINCE THE DRIVE UP TO Los Alamos and the return ride down its orange cliff approaches, when the Santa Clara Valley opens up like a panoramic canvas of endless blue sky and bluer sierras, the river course below like a string of emeralds set in silver and displayed on the ruffled fabric of ochre deserts. These ruffles were bluffs and mesas of every shape and hue scattered about for miles and ages.

The Colonel was a landscape painter of sorts as well as an amateur geologist, and therefore interested in bits of history connected with each phase of the landscape. The driver of the car was keeping him supplied with such items, as though he knew the intimate story of each rock and every turn of the river. He, too, was in military uniform, but wearing the small crosses of a chaplain. His rank was lower as were, decidedly, his age and weight. The olive-drab caps and blouses, and the many-hued campaign

ribbons over their hearts, were the single point of resemblance
between the two men.

But though they had met for the first time in Santa Fe that
morning, they understood each other; that is, the younger man
knew what words to use in pointing out a cliff or basalt, or naming
the color of a sandstone fault, and finally, after they reached
bottom and crossed the river, in recounting the strategy used by a
Spanish Captain-General of long ago in dislodging the Tewa
Indians from the Black Mesa of San Ildefonso to their left.

This mesa looked like the gray-blue uneven pate of some
gigantic elephant, and the Colonel spoke for the first time in
twenty minutes. It reminded him, he said, of another bluff on a far
Pacific island, as well as the one purpose of this his first visit to
New Mexico.

He had forgotten the soldier boy all this while, but now the
scape and sky, triggered by the sight of that bluff, brought him
back to Cash, especially the unbelievably wide and blue sky. For
Cash had always talked with a touch of homesickness about his
blue sky back home. He believed the lad now.

"Are you quite sure where Cash's mother lives?" he finally
asked, swiveling his big weight toward the driver.

His companion nodded and said they had to go on for several
more miles to the east, to the foothills of the great sierras, which
now were a deep velvet green. What had appeared like a short
skip, when he pointed out the place from Los Alamos, was actually a distance of twelve miles or so.

"If they had dropped that thing a couple of months before
they did, Cash wouldn't have died," the Colonel said, after the
driver had mentioned Los Alamos. "Poor kid. He would have
seen this place, this sky, again."

"You must have really liked the fellow, Colonel, to come all
the way out here. He must have been a top soldier."

"Well, yes and no. In fact, he was a poor soldier when you
come to think of it, and still he was of the best, the very best. And
he was a likeable character. You couldn't stay mad at Cash for
long."

"Cash? That's a strange name for a boy from these parts. Was
it a nickname?"

"Not that I know of, Padre. That was the name in his file—Cash Atencio. Well, he was in my battalion since the division was activated at the start of the war. He started training with us, and was with us until the day he died. You know how one gets to know and like the men who have been with the outfit for years."

The chaplain nodded.

"And Cash was no ordinary soldier, in the sense that he'd fade in the ranks of a company, or even a whole battalion. From the start I noticed Cash. Besides, he showed signs of leadership and quick judgment in field problems. He got to be a sergeant several times."

"Several times?"

"Yes. I had to bust him down to a buck private on different occasions, and each time he climbed up to corporal, and at last to top sergeant. But then he would get busted again. In fact, he was a private, and I had him for my jeep driver, when they got him."

"Colonel, how could he have been a born leader and a likeable character, and still be such a sad sack?"

"Well, let's put it this way. He had brains and other qualities, but didn't realize it. He had all the makings of a good non-com, and let me say that he had no basically grave faults that would call for court-martial. And he was a very religious guy. Never missed chapel on Sundays, and he used to wear a big five-inch cross, you know—yes, crucifix—on the same chain with his dog-tags. Its weight made it drop out of his fatigue jacket while at work, but I never heard of any soldier kidding him about it.

"But all of a sudden Cash would take off without leave, or he would overstay his furlough without notifying his captain. Or he would get drunk downtown on a couple of beers and wreck up the joint, and then resist arrest when the MP's nabbed him. Each time it was a formal military police charge, and so I had to discipline him. But Cash never got mad or sulked. In fact, it was I who got raving mad when I lectured him and pleaded with him like a father, only to see that he could not grasp what I was driving at. I could not drive into his head the idea of responsibility—that's it, responsibility. And that's what most of these Mexican boys lacked."

The driver colored a trifle but grinned to himself. "Pardon

me, Colonel," he said. "But let me inform you that Cash and your other boys from these parts were not Mexican."

The older officer's jaw fell at the unexpected remark.

"New Mexico was a Spanish colony long before New England, and existed for two centuries and a quarter before there ever was a Republic of Mexico. Hence, '*Old* Mexico' is a mis-statement. And she belonged to the Mexican Republic for only twenty-five years, while she has been a part of the United States now for a hundred years."

"But the people are part Indian, aren't they? Cash looked a little bit Indian."

"One cannot go by looks alone, sir, especially with the Latin races. But even if Cash did have a remote strain of Indian, which is no disgrace, this does not make him an Indian. The famed Will Rogers, whom you mentioned this morning as distant kin of yours, was a quarter Indian. Does this make him a Mexican? Of course not. This is because the word 'Mexican' denotes a nationality and a culture, and a very superior one. A citizen of Mexico, whether he be white, red, black, or mixed, is a true Mexican and proud of it. He might make social distinctions, but not racial ones. It is we reputedly democratic Americans who make them, and incorrect ones at that."

"I'm sorry," the Colonel apologized. "You see, that's what I have always heard. Only this morning, at the hotel, a Santa Fe gentleman referred to these people as Mexicans."

The chaplain was laughing. "I am not blaming you, sir, just explaining, just as we were discussing geology, history, and art a while back."

As the Colonel remained gloomily silent, the driver chuckled and spoke again.

"Let's get in a bit of psychology also. It is only here in New Mexico that some people can *think* the word 'Mexican' and at the same time pronounce the altogether distinct word 'Spanish.' It's a hard trick with many a slip. And do you know that we priests are the worst offenders?"

"No!" the Colonel started. "That's strange."

The chaplain could feel that his companion had regained his composure, now that he shared his *faux pas* with others.

The Colonel did feel more at ease now, but at the same time he began wondering if Cash had resented the term. He could not recall a single instance, but it might go some way towards explaining his irresponsible outbursts. The last time was at Seattle, when he almost missed the boat for the islands. Not that he was afraid to go. Cash was afraid of nothing. He simply went off the restricted area, wrecked a small bar and restaurant downtown, and was dragged up the gangplank by the military police at the last moment. From then on Sergeant Cash was a private until the day he died.

That day was a dark and muggy one, just like most days in the tropics during the rainy season, and especially during action. It seemed as though constant artillery barrages and aerial bombings tended to shake the heavens loose. The regiment had been detailed to take the northern tip of the big island, and had done so after almost a week of heavy fighting and mopping up. The regimental commander was killed by a sniper's bullet on the second day, and the Colonel, then a light Colonel, was removed from his battalion to take his place. After the main action was over, he remembered Cash down in the battalion and had him transferred up to regimental headquarters.

"He was a wonderful driver in all kinds of bad roads, including axle-deep mud. Besides, he knew what I wanted without having to say much. That's the advantage of working and training together for a long time. Cash had done well during combat, his captain told me, and was on the list of those to be recommended for decoration. My intention was to use his driving abilities for the time being, and then restore his sergeant's stripes when the medals were dished out.

"Well, it was one of those muggy days, as I was saying, when I decided to inspect some forward gun positions on the other side of Elephant Butte, a lone mountain bluff on our end of the island. This was the name the men gave it, only they mispronounced the second word. Which made no difference as far as looks were concerned. It appeared very much like that Black Mesa we passed, except that it was all green, the bits of steep ground with grass and bush, the bare rock with lichen. Between us and the bluff lay a couple miles of dense swampy jungle, not open country like this where you can see a jackrabbit leap and hop for a mile. And the sky was a heavy gray, like lead.

"I was kidding Cash about missing his blue skies as the jeep roared and squirmed over the narrow raised road of black muck, always managing to keep from slipping down among the thick stands of dripping palm and bamboo on either side, when more than a dozen enemy soldiers broke out of concealment and blocked the road ahead. I was sitting in front next to Cash, my adjutant on the seat in back.

"Before either of us could say a word, Cash threw the jeep in reverse and roared madly backward for several yards, while those monkeys began shooting at us. The adjutant and I just got our guns out of their holsters when we were catapulted head over heels into a murky trench of mud and reeds. Then the jeep roared back on the roadbed and made angrily for the roadblock ahead. It was then that I realized that Cash had purposely dumped us off to carry out a plan of his.

"How he got that jeep to clamber back on the road was miracle enough. How he went through that ambush and past it without getting hit was another wonder. Of course, they leaped aside when he rushed past them. Once beyond them, he stopped the vehicle astride the road, took off the rifle strapped to the jeep's side, and began peppering them, using the jeep as a bunker. The adjutant and I wanted to do our part, but the two pistols were in deep water beyond retrieving.

"I saw them toss grenades at the jeep, and suddenly it blew up with a couple of explosions. By the time the smoke cleared away they had slunk back into the jungle.

"We didn't dare move, without weapons, and we lay still in the reeds and palmettos. One of our patrols had started our way on hearing the shooting, but when they reached us the heavens opened up with bucketfuls. When the storm was over we went cautiously to examine the wrecked jeep. But Cash was not there."

The chaplain's car slowed down, veered off the main road and rolled down a short distance among some clumps of bluish-green sagebrush, to stop before a small adobe house dozing cool and quiet under the glossy umbrella of a giant conttonwood.

"Is this the place?" the Colonel asked, shocked out of the reverie which his narrative had conjured up.

"That's what it said on the mailbox by the roadside," the chaplain answered, going over to knock on the low blue door.

For a spell there was no answer, nor any noise, only the very slight but sharp rustle of big leaves overhead. It was like being in a painting, the Colonel felt. Then the door opened quietly, to frame a young mother with a baby on her arm.

Her long black hair and plain dress were disheveled, and the light skin of her bare arms and face glowed with the clean flush that comes from working over hot water. The child and its dress were spotless. When the chaplain spoke to her in Spanish, asking for Cash's mother, she replied in English, first excusing her appearance, then bidding them come into the house. She was Cash's sister. Her husband was up in the mountains getting wood. Her mother was at the neighbor's down the road. While they made themselves at home she would run down and fetch the old lady.

The Colonel began to feel a strange comfort in the room. He soon found the answer in the wavy floor, which felt like packed earth that was padded over with neat rag-rugs of every size and shape—and in the uneven flow of the white-washed walls from floor to equally uneven cloth ceiling. He had felt the same comfort in a campaign tent; it was the round touch of mother earth, of one's own mother. He was about to expound to his companion about the true functionality and hominess of rounded uneven surfaces, as against unorganic modernistic angles, when an old picture on the end wall caught and held his eye.

"Say! That's the strangest way of dressing Christ on the Cross!" he almost shouted, getting up and pacing over to examine it more closely.

It was a two-foot wooden panel, uneven like the walls, with a few thin cracks running up and down with the grain, which was almost visible underneath the age-darkened pigments. The main figure stood out because of the simple black outlines, without depth, like a child's effort or one of those modernistic French paintings—only not so impudent and glaring. At the foot of the cross were painted six miniature soldiers. The first had a drum, the rest stood at dress parade with their little muskets.

But the main crucified figure, in military uniform like the tiny soldiers beneath, still clamored for an explanation.

The Padre was laughing quietly to himself, and finally began to explain.

"That is not Christ on the Cross, sir, but the figure of a once very popular saint in New Mexico, by the name of San Acacio. Acacio! That explains Cash's name. I'll bet you anything it was his grandfather's name, and his father's also."

The Colonel's face went suddenly drawn and colorless as he leaned for a moment against a rug-covered chest that stood below the picture. When he spoke again his voice was hoarse and trembling.

"This is a most uncanny thing, Padre. I hadn't finished telling you about Cash's death. I said we didn't find his body by the wrecked jeep after the rainstorm was over. But hours later some of our men did find him—like this." And he pointed to the saint.

"He lay face-up on a steep slope of Elephant Hill with arms stretched out, and a bayonet through each hand pinning him to the ground. That crucifix he always wore was hanging out of his open denim jacket. Perhaps it gave those demons the idea. My theory is that they dragged him over to the hill during the storm. I only hope that he was already dead."

He contemplated the painting before speaking again.

"This '*San Cashio*' must have been a Spanish officer. He's wearing a colonel's uniform of Spanish troops in the early 1800's—epaulets, black sailor hat of the period, scarlet sash over light blue blouse, and long white trousers stuck in campaign boots. Only the boots are more like a cowboy's."

"They were military boots originally, sir," the chaplain offered, pointing out where a much later hand had drawn curved tops on each boot and added the curleycue decorations affected by Western footwear. No, he further explained to the Colonel, San Acacio was not a colonel in the Spanish army of the nineteenth century, but this uniform did date the painting itself. It must have been in this Atencio family for three generations or more. San Acacio himself, or St. Achatius, was a Roman army officer of the fourth century, serving in Asia Minor. Because he and his men had become Christians, they were all crucified like their Master. The little soldiers could represent his executioners, or even his own soldiers before they themselves were nailed to crosses.

"And Cash was one of his little soldiers," the Colonel said, pounding his fist forcefully.

Just then they heard footsteps at the door, and turned around to see the young woman with her child. In front of them was a tiny wisp of an old lady in a long black dress. Her small round face, netted with wrinkles, and the clasped hands in front of her small bodice, were browned by thousands of sunlit days. Her white hair was swept back tightly into a neat ball of cotton on the back of her neck. Her large brown eyes were guilelessly clear, like a little girl's, yet rich with the sweet pains of a lifetime bravely borne.

This was what the Colonel saw while the chaplain made the usual introductions and explained the unusual visit, and then proceeded to tell the old woman (all in Spanish) about her son's death in the islands. Meanwhile, the sister in the background was crying softly to herself.

At one moment, when some invisible light suffused the aged mother's features as a quiet smile formed on her lips, the Colonel put his hand on the chaplain's shoulder and interrupted him.

"Padre, be sure not to tell how we found him."

"But I just did, sir."

The old lady looked up at the Colonel, but spoke to the chaplain: "Tell the gentleman how proud I am to know that my son died like the Lord and like his patron saint."

With this she took the hand of the Colonel, who had taken out a ribboned metal to pin on her dress, and kissed it reverently. Then she took the decoration from his helpless fingers, glided over to the *santo,* and stuck the open pin in a crack over San Acacio's heart. It covered most of his blue blouse.